henshin

ken niimura

1. no good

12:53
12:57

WHERE ARE MY GLASSES...
OH, HERE THEY ARE! YOUR UNCLE IS GOING SENILE. HAHA!

NAT-CHAN, DID YOU LIKE SPAGHETTI?

NEAPOLITAN'S MY FAVORITE.

LET'S GO IN.

EMAILING YOUR BOYFRIEND BACK HOME?

POOR GUY. YOU'LL BE GETTING LOTS OF ATTENTION HERE. YOU MIGHT EVEN END UP WITH SEVERAL TOKYO BOYFRIENDS. HAHA!

OH, TO BE YOUNG AGAIN!

YOU CAN STAY AT OUR HOUSE AS LONG AS YOU WANT, UNTIL YOU FIND A NEW SCHOOL AND AN APARTMENT, OK?
I HAVEN'T SEEN YOU IN SO LONG, I'M SO HAPPY YOU CAME TO TOKYO.

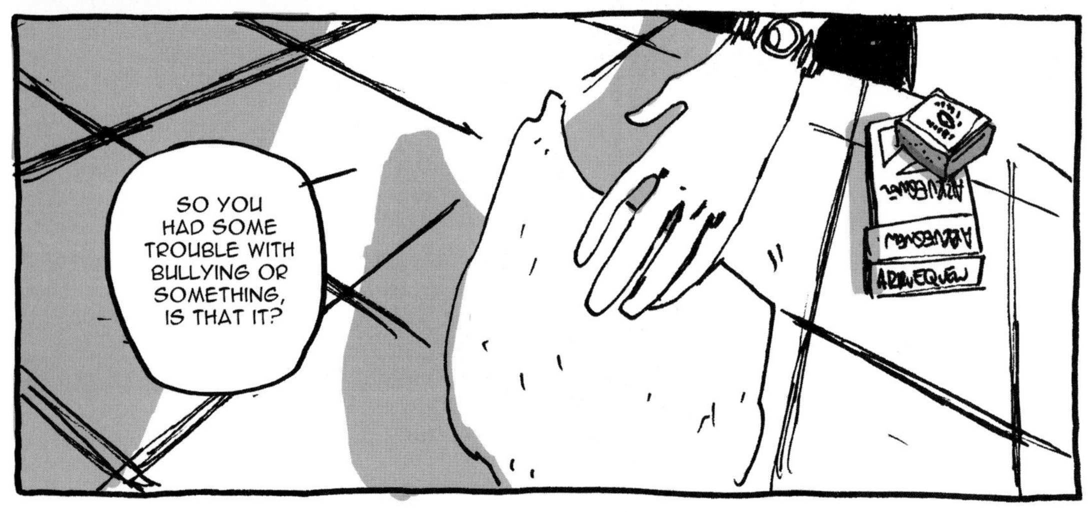
SO YOU HAD SOME TROUBLE WITH BULLYING OR SOMETHING, IS THAT IT?

WELL, THERE'S NOTHING TO WORRY ABOUT. NOBODY KNOWS YOU HERE.
I COMPLETELY UNDERSTAND. I HAD LOTS GOING ON TOO, WHEN I WAS YOUNG.
SO I'M ON YOUR SIDE.

は会
ショップ・メイト

NAT-CHAN.

WAIT HERE FOR ME, OK?
おもち

OK, LET'S GO. I STILL HAVE SOME ERRANDS TO RUN.

THANKS FOR THE PURCHASE, SIR.

COME ON, NAT-CHAN.

2 CV
CITROEN

I HAVE TO TAKE CARE OF SOMETHING, DO YOU MIND?

I'LL BE RIGHT BACK.

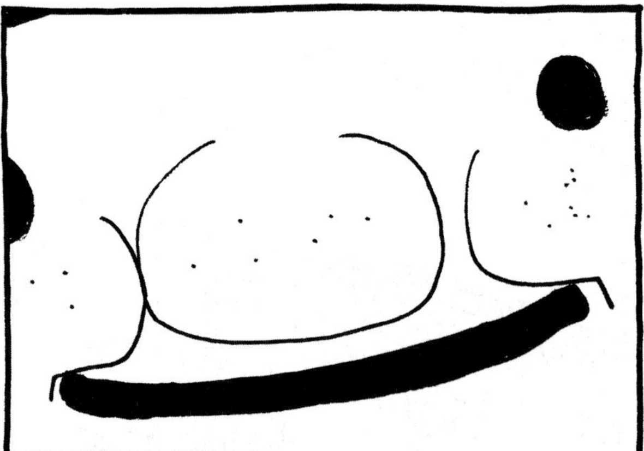

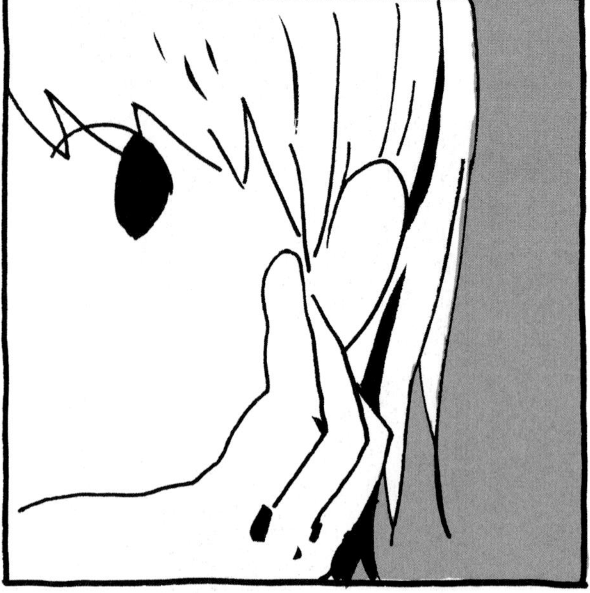

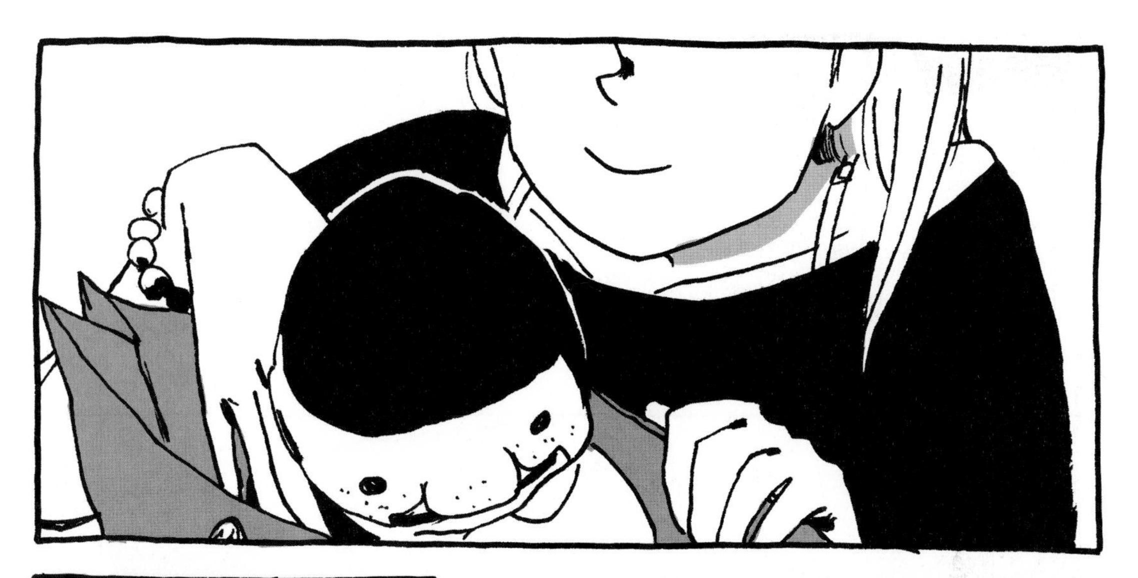

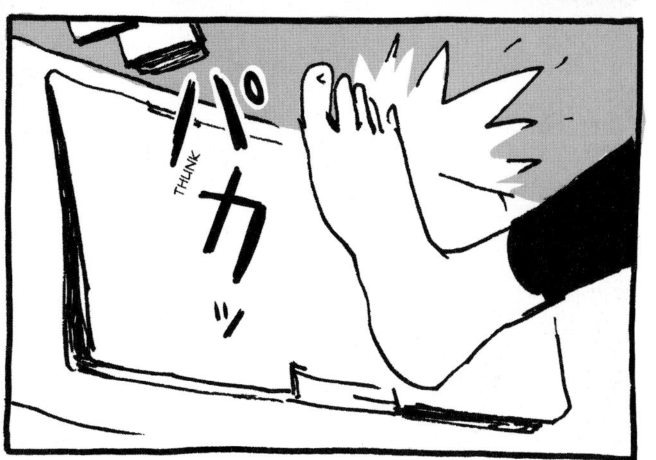
パカッ
THLINK

NO ENTRY
禁止

BANG

MAN, I'M REALLY LOSING MY MARBLES.

HOW COULD I FORGET MY GUN IN THE CAR?

NAT-CHAN,
WOULD YOU MIND CALLING YOUR AUNT? THERE'S A PHONE IN THE GLOVE COMPARTMENT.

TELL HER WE'RE RUNNING LATE.

THIS ISN'T THE FIRST TIME YOU'VE KILLED SOMEONE, IS IT?
DON'T WORRY. I THINK IT'S BETTER TO BULLY THAN BE BULLIED.
I'LL ALWAYS BE YOUR ALLY.

AFTER ALL, WE'RE FAMILY.

2. kitty and me

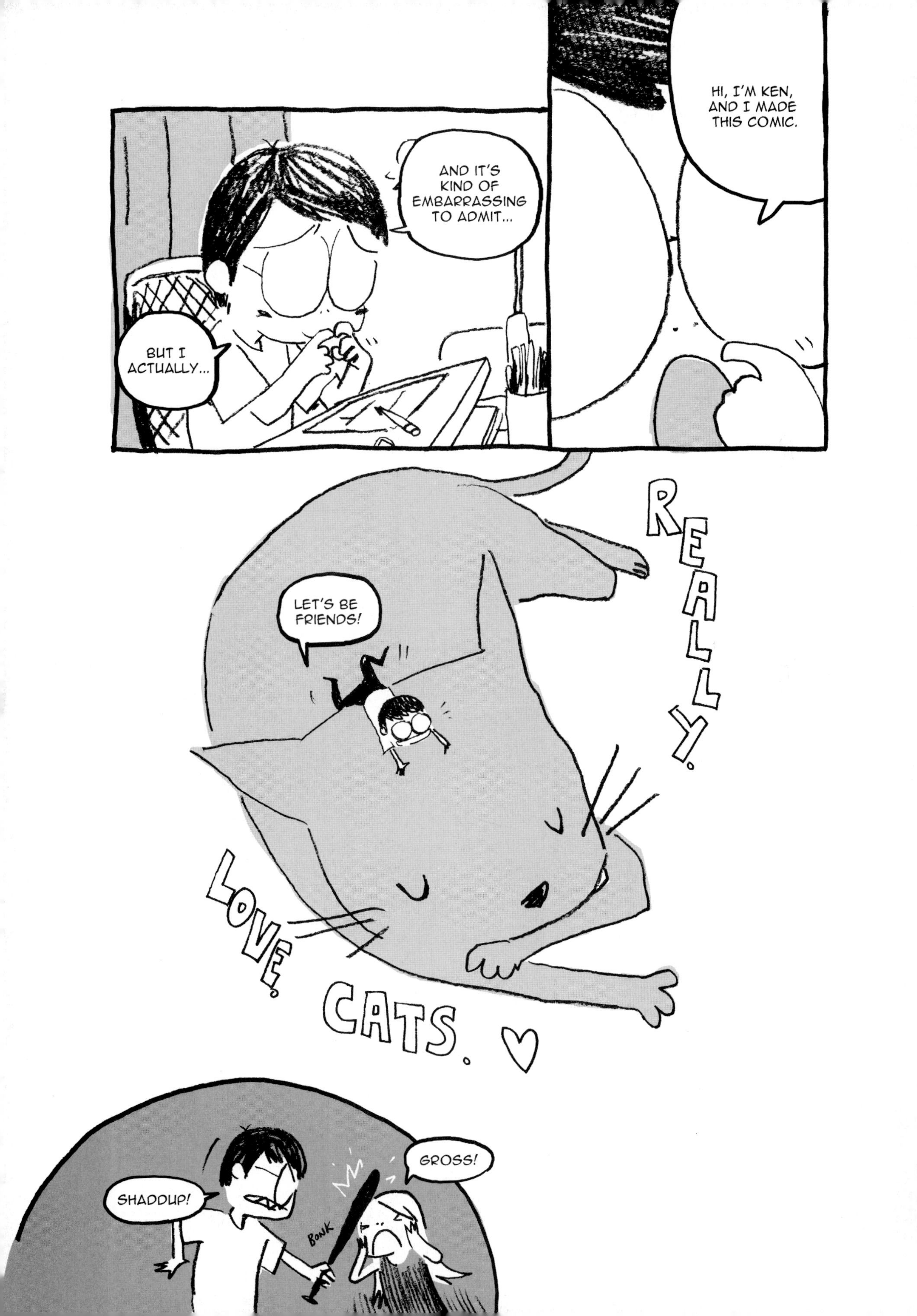
HI, I'M KEN, AND I MADE THIS COMIC.
AND IT'S KIND OF EMBARRASSING TO ADMIT...
BUT I ACTUALLY...
REALLY.
LOVE. CATS. ♥
LET'S BE FRIENDS!
GROSS!
SHADDUP!
BONK

TWO YEARS AGO, I RENTED AN APARTMENT AND AGREED TO LOOK AFTER MY LANDLORD'S CAT.

I STARTED WANTING A CAT OF MY OWN...
CHAMPAGNE!

SO... SO CUUUTE!!!
BUT I COULDN'T AFFORD IT, SO I'D JUST WATCH CAT VIDEOS ONLINE.
THEN ONE DAY, MY WISH CAME TRUE...

I'M A CAT OWNER NOW.
THUD
AAAAHH!!!
♪
WHAT! THERE WAS CAT POOP IN YOUR CORRIDOR?
OWW...

YEP, AND THAT WAS THE THIRD TIME.
NO, IT WAS DEFINITELY A CAT.
A SWEET LITTLE CAT THAT WANTS TO BE FRIENDS WITH ME.
BUT WHAT IF IT WAS A STRANGER WHO'D HAD AN ACCIDENT?
OR IF IT WAS MAGIC POOP FROM THE FUTURE, (YOU KNOW, LIKE *DORAEMON*).

NICE. ME TOO.
SPEAKING OF POOP, I HAD A GREAT ONE THIS MORNING!
UHH...
AND, TODAY I DISCOVERED A WAY TO DIVIDE ALL HUMANS INTO TWO GROUPS.
DO TELL.
A: THOSE WHO CAN TAKE A DUMP ANYWHERE.
B: THOSE WHO CAN ONLY GO AT HOME.
BRING IT ON
PARDON ME
I'M DEFINITELY A "B".
OOH, THAT'S GENIUS.
YOU GUYS ARE HOPELESS...
NICE

A FEW YEARS AGO, I WAS OUT IN THE COUNTRYSIDE...
A... HOLE?
AND THE TOILETS WERE SO BAD I HAD TO HOLD IT FOR A WEEK.

HOW MUCH LONGER...?
THIS IS AWFUL...
MY FRIENDS WERE THE SAME AS ME. WE LOOKED UP REAL WASHROOMS AND DROVE TO THE CLOSEST ONE, AT A SUPERMARKET, AN HOUR AWAY.
WE MADE IT!
ANY TIME WE GET TOGETHER, WE REMINISCE ABOUT THAT TOILET.
THIS IS WHAT WE CALL AN "EMOTIONAL BOND."
EXACTLY.

I FEEL THE MOST AT EASE WHEN I'M AT HOME, LEISURELY READING A BOOK.
AND WHEN I MOVE INTO A NEW PLACE, ONCE I CAN COMFORTABLY USE THE TOILET, I KNOW I'VE MADE MY HOUSE A HOME.
HOME SWEET HOME...

IF I FELT AT HOME STAYING AT A FRIEND'S PLACE, I WOULD SAY...
I'VE HAD A LOVELY TIME RELIEVING MYSELF IN YOUR TOILET.
WORDS OF PRAISE.
WELL THAT'S JUST... I'M DELIGHTED...

BUT THE ONLY TOILET THAT'S A SACRED PLACE IS THE ONE IN THE HOUSE WHERE I GREW UP.
WELCOME HOME, MASTER.
WE HAVE A LONG HISTORY...

WAIT A SECOND!
WHAT HAPPENED TO THE CAT STORY?
SHHH!
WE'RE IN A MAN'S FANTASY! DON'T RUIN IT.

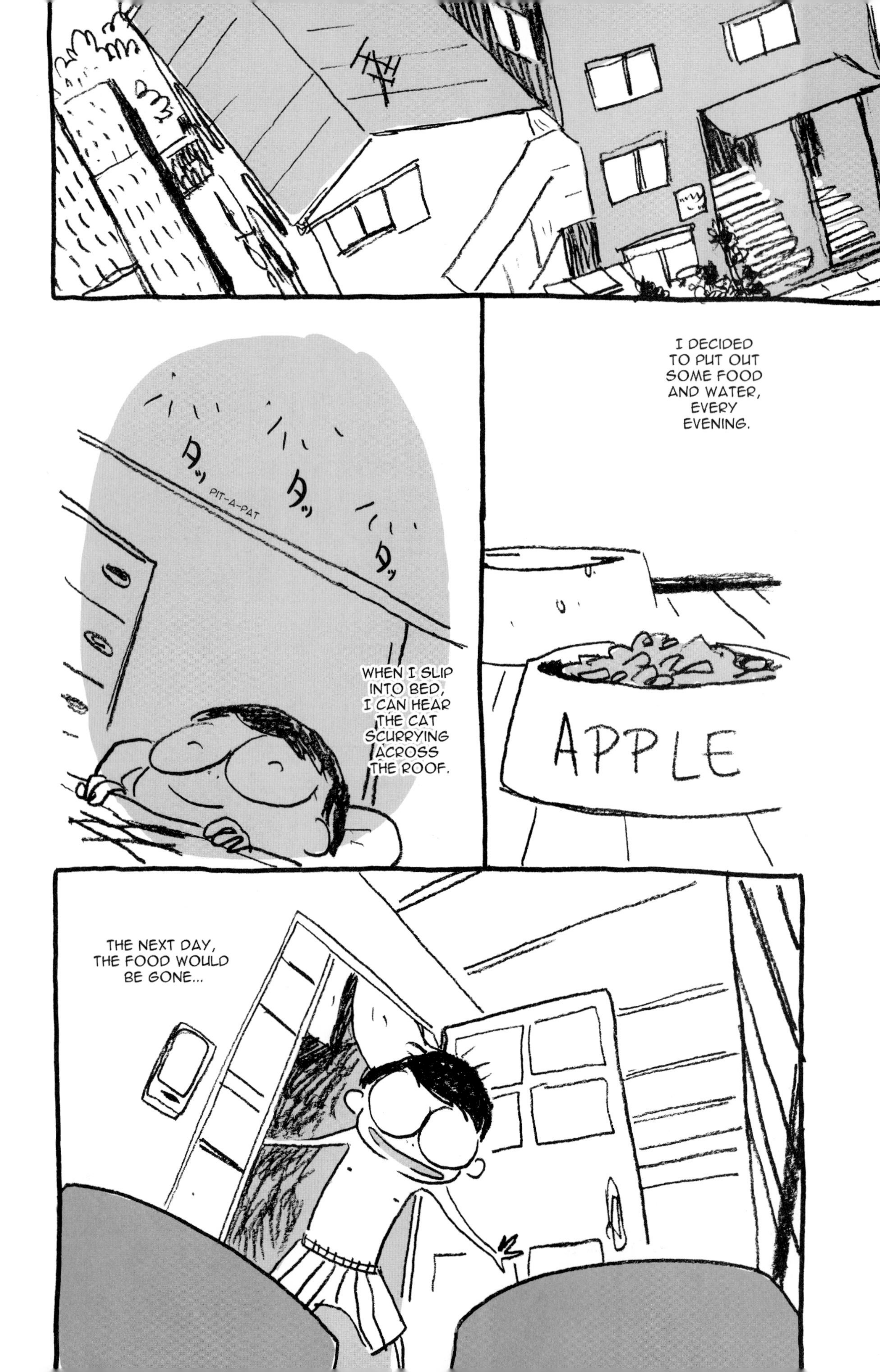
タッ
PIT-A-PAT
タッ
タッ
WHEN I SLIP INTO BED, I CAN HEAR THE CAT SCURRYING ACROSS THE ROOF.
I DECIDED TO PUT OUT SOME FOOD AND WATER, EVERY EVENING.
APPLE
THE NEXT DAY, THE FOOD WOULD BE GONE...

AND THERE WOULD BE POOP IN THE SAME PLACE AS ALWAYS.
IT'S LIKE TALKING TO A FRIEND IN A SECRET LANGUAGE.
THERE'S NO PLACE LIKE THE FAMILY HOME.

CLACK
OWW...
THUD

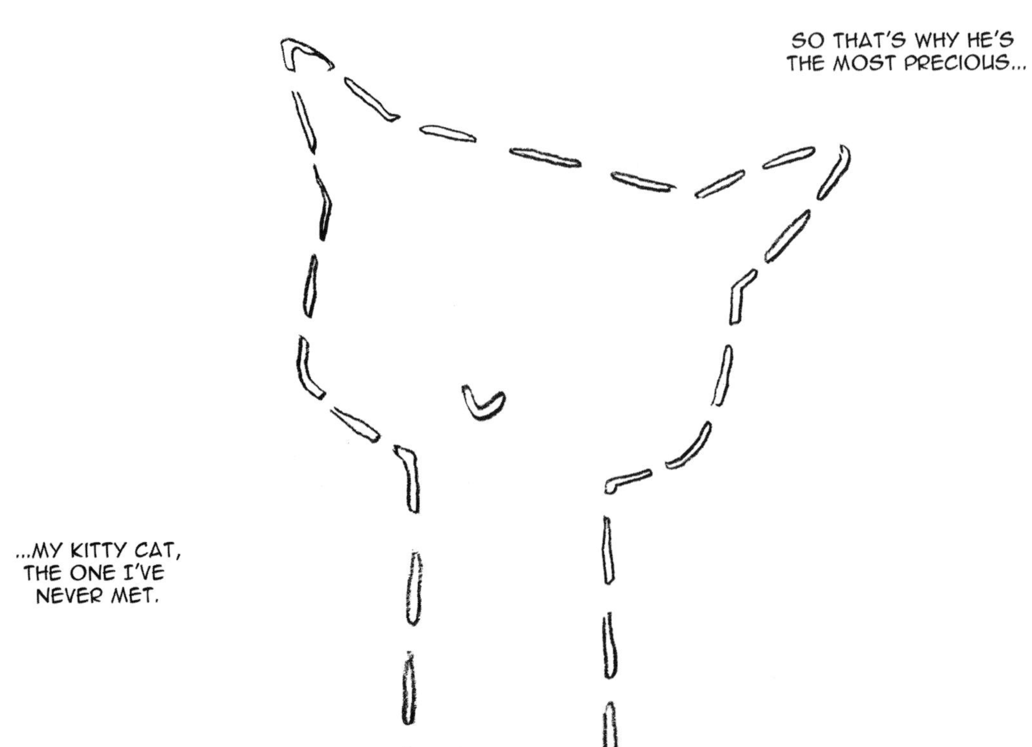
SO THAT'S WHY HE'S
THE MOST PRECIOUS...
...MY KITTY CAT,
THE ONE I'VE
NEVER MET.

3. last train

"THE LAST TRAIN
IS ABOUT TO LEAVE
THE STATION."

entrance
SMACK
I SAID STOP IT!
EEK!
LET GO!

FLOOSH
EXCUSE ME.
Beep

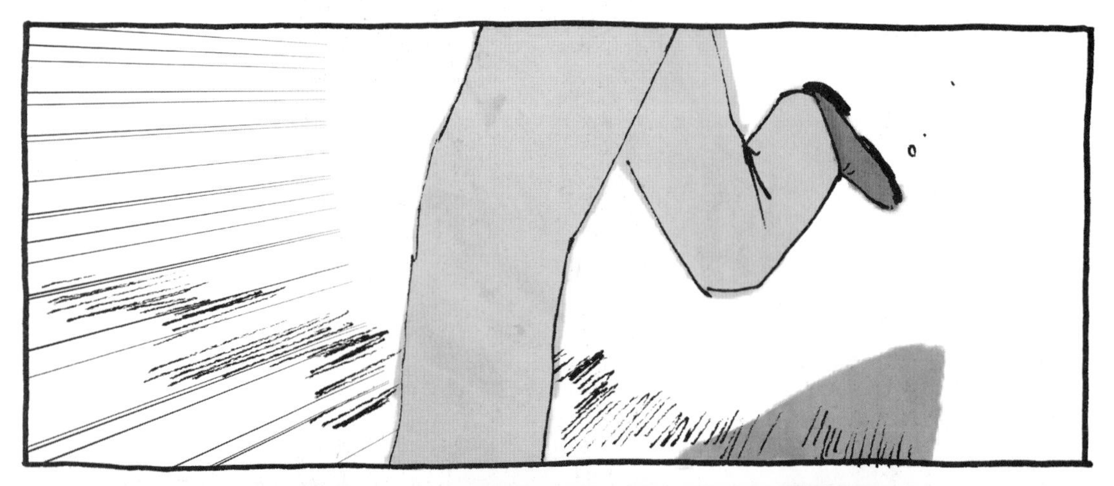

NEW ALBUM
TRAVELING
MY FIRST TIME MISSING THE LAST TRAIN... HOW PATHETIC...
I SHOULD'VE PASSED ON THE PORK CUTLET.

WHAT DO PEOPLE DO UNTIL MORNING?
EXCUSE ME.

JUST NOW, BY THE TICKET GATES...
THANK YOU.

OH, IT'S NO PROBLEM.

I KNOW A GOOD PLACE AROUND THE CORNER.
CARE TO JOIN ME?

WELLP...
UM..

IT'S BEEN A WHILE SINCE I'VE GONE DRINKING... WHAT THE HECK. NOT LIKE I HAVE ANYTHING BETTER TO DO.

I WORK CLOSE BY, SO I KNOW THE GOLDEN-GAI AREA PRETTY WELL.
IT BETTER NOT BE ONE OF THOSE RIP-OFF JOINTS... I MEAN, I'D BE WILLING TO BUY DRINKS, BUT...

WHAT DO YOU DO?
I DON'T WANT TO GET DRUGGED AND ROBBED...

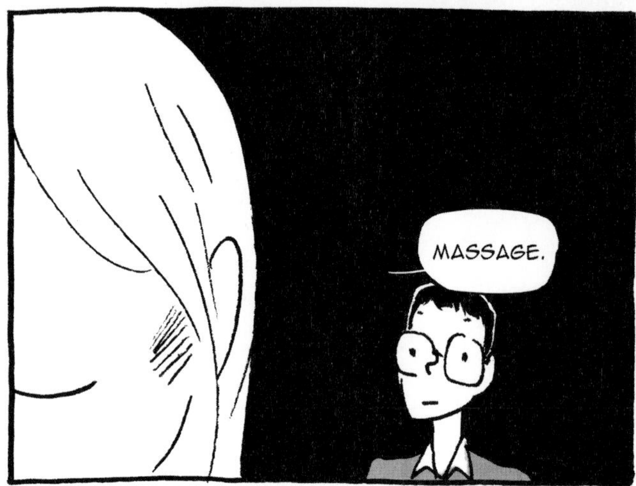

MASSAGE.

OH, YOU MEAN WITH HAPPY ENDINGS?
I CAN SEE WHY THAT'D PISS OFF YOUR BOYFRIEND.
HAHA.

OH, I'M SO SORRY, SLIP OF THE TONGUE.
YOU'VE GOTTA BE KIDDING ME.

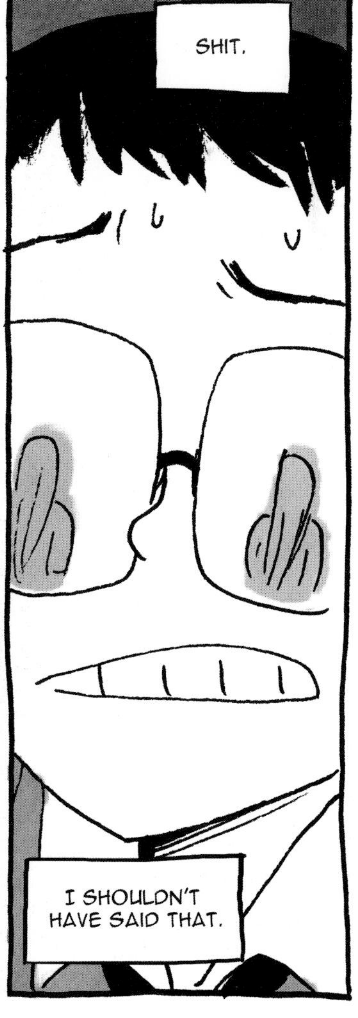
SHIT.
I SHOULDN'T HAVE SAID THAT.

うま

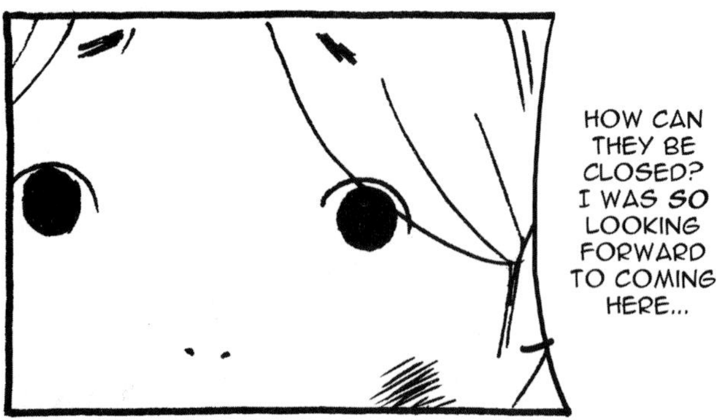
HOW CAN THEY BE CLOSED? I WAS **SO** LOOKING FORWARD TO COMING HERE...

WELL...

...I HAVE AN IDEA.

CHEERS!

PHEW!
BEER IS THE BEST!

OH!
HUH?

I'M ONLY ON MY SECOND ONE, BUT I'M ALREADY FEELING IT. AH WELL.

CAN YOU HEAR
THE MUSIC?

I HAVE NO
IDEA WHAT'S
GOING ON,
BUT...

SHE'S A GODDESS...

C'MON AN'
GET UP-AH!

IT'S NO FUN BY MYSELF.
OH, PLEASE, STAND UP!
UH... UH OH...
URP

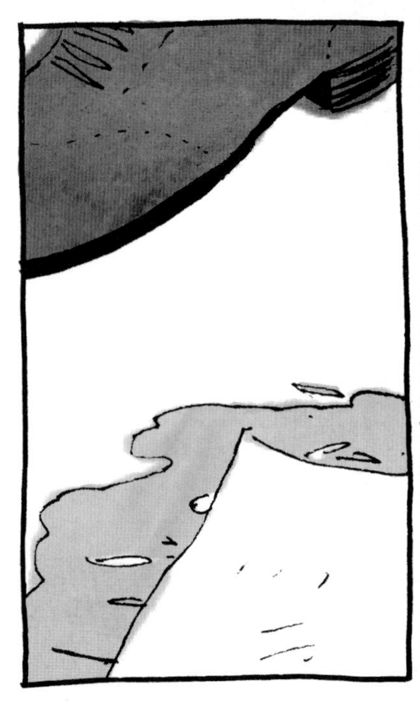

NO WAY...

DO YOU HAVE A MINUTE?

UH, YES.

YOU'RE WEARING THE SAME CLOTHES AS YESTERDAY. THAT'S UNEXPECTED.
HEH...

I BROUGHT YOU THE FORM FOR YOUR ID CARD RENEWAL.

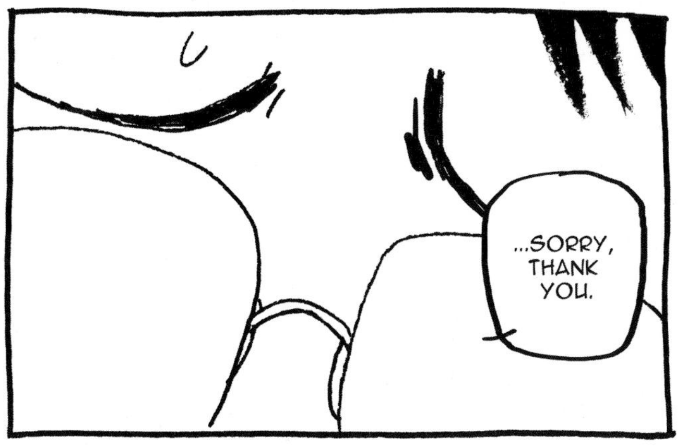
...SORRY, THANK YOU.

HM?

DARUMA DRAFT BEER
DARUMA

4. the bully bros

NAOKI! GET DRESSED!
WHO'S COMING OVER, ANYWAY?

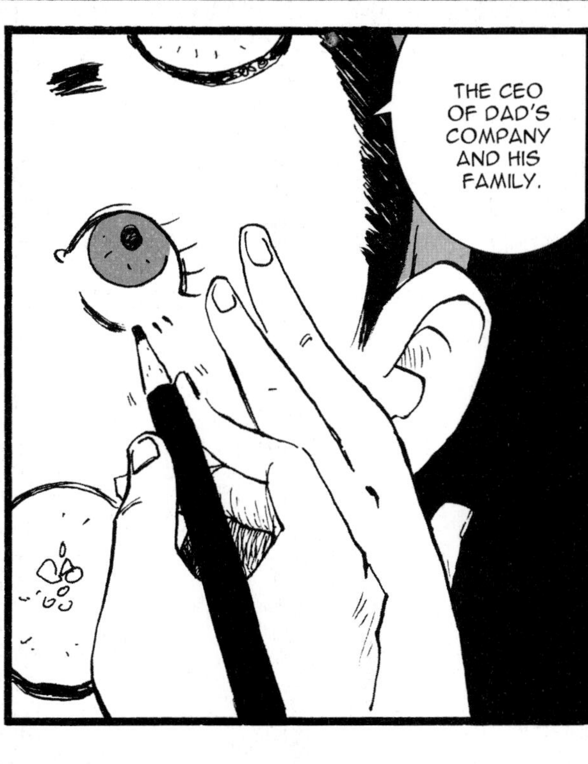
THE CEO OF DAD'S COMPANY AND HIS FAMILY.

WHAT? SO THERE'S GONNA BE KIDS TOO?
I TOLD YOU, THE TWINS.

AND SO...
POP

IF ALL GOES WELL, DAD MIGHT LAND A PROMOTION.

YOU HAVE TO BE A GOOD BOY TODAY.

HEY!
NAOKI! STOP IT!
POW

WE CAN COUNT ON NAOKI TO BE GOOD.

BUT...
HOW MANY TIMES DO I HAVE TO TELL YOU NOT TO DO THAT?
WHAT ARE YOU GOING TO DO IF STRANGERS CATCH YOU?

HONEY!
POW
RIGHT, BUDDY?

I'M SICK AND TIRED OF MOVING AND STARTING OVER!

THINGS WERE GOING SO WELL UNTIL NOW!
DON'T SCREW IT UP, OR ELSE!

GOT IT? BOTH OF YOU?

ピンポーン
DING DONG

UH...
OH, IT'S NOTHING, REALLY.

HI THERE!
OH, A CAKE! YOU SHOULDN'T HAVE!
THANKS FOR HAVING US.

HEY! WHERE ARE YOUR MANNERS?
SUP.
SUP.
THAT'S IT. GOOD BOYS.

NAOKI...
CAN YOU
HEAR ME?
THIS IS YOUR
MOTHER...

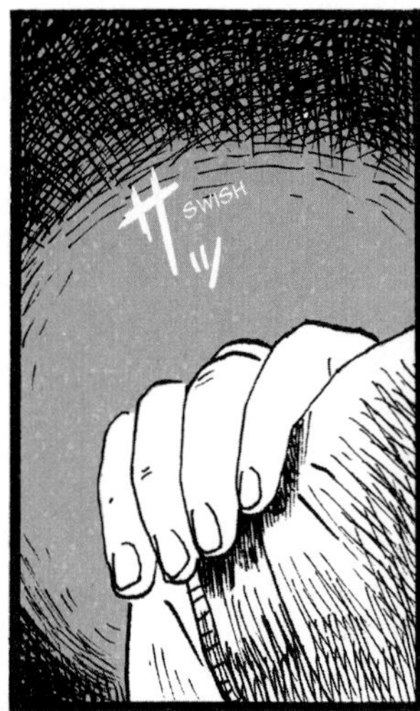
SWISH

HEY.

BE FRIENDLY
WITH THEM.

AND DO
NOT USE "IT."

BWAHAHA!

IT'S FOR THE BEST, FOR ALL CONCERNED.

...
MOVE IT, YOU IDIOT!

MY TURN!
SHOVE OFF!

NAOKI! SAVE ME!
NO, SAVE ME!

I WANNA GO.
LET'S GO.
UM, WAIT!

CHECK IT OUT, IT'S ARAKAWA RIVER!

THE RIVER'S DANGEROUS...
UM...
WHAT.

SO LET'S GO TO THE ARCADE OVER THERE.

YEAH!

LET US DO WHAT WE WANT, OR WE'LL TELL OUR DAD.
HEE HEE!

タッ
タッ
タッ
RUN RUN RUN

WHAT IS THIS, A SECRET FORT?
WHAT A JOKE!

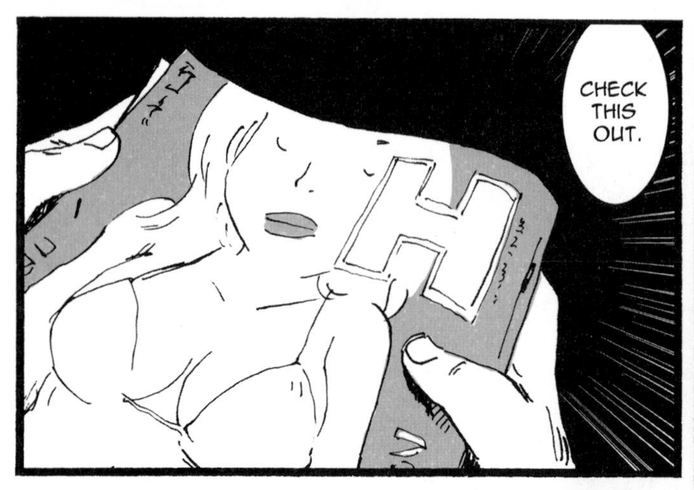
CHECK THIS OUT.

LET'S GO BACK...
HEY.

THIS IS OUR DOMAIN.
SCREW OFF.
GRR...
WHY YOU LITTLE...

GIVE THAT BACK!
STOP!
SWISH

WE'RE SORRY.
WE... WE'LL NOT BE ON YOUR WAY.

WELL...

HE WANTS US TO FORGIVE THEM.

GIVE US ALL YOUR MONEY.
OR ELSE...

OWW!

CRAP...

I COULD SAVE THEM IF I USED "IT"... BUT THEN THEY'LL FIND OUT, AND MOM WILL KILL ME.

...BUT THIS COULD GET MESSY...

WHAT DO I DO...?

WHAT'S YOUR PROBLEM?
PAY UP!

PF

PF

PF
PF
PF

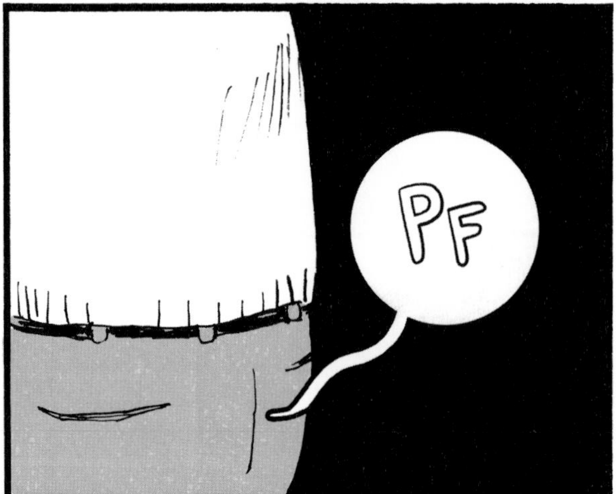
PF

HUH?

YOU THINK THIS IS FUNNY? ASSHOLE!
AH!

パキッ
THUD

H...
HEY.

WHAT HAPPENED?
THUD

GRRR...

BRING IT ON!

CRAP. NOW EVERYONE KNOWS...

UM, NO, I, NOTHING, THAT WAS...
I DON'T KNOW WHAT YOU'RE...

HEY. WHAT WAS...

THAT WAS THE GROSSEST FART EVER!
AWESOME!
EH?

I MIGHT BE IN THE CLEAR.

WE'RE LEAVING, KIDS!

THANKS FOR EVERYTHING TODAY.
MOVE IT!
04-13

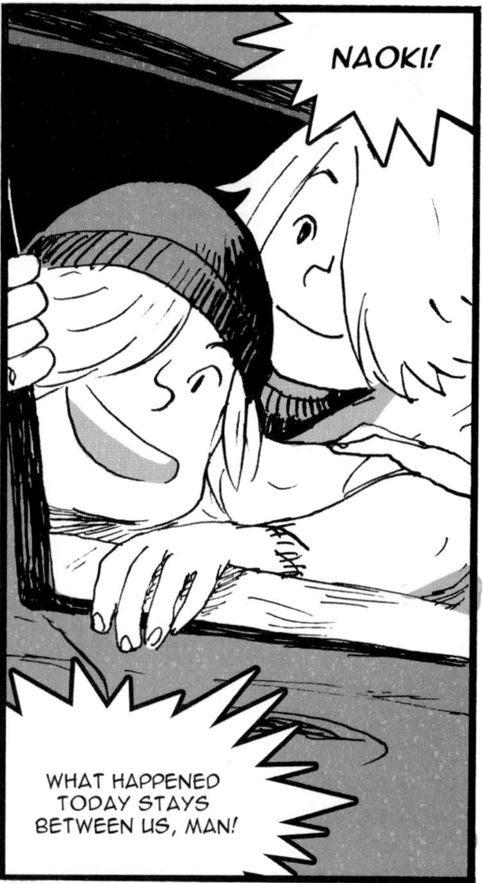
NAOKI!
WHAT HAPPENED TODAY STAYS BETWEEN US, MAN!

YOU CAN COUNT ON ME.

NOPE.

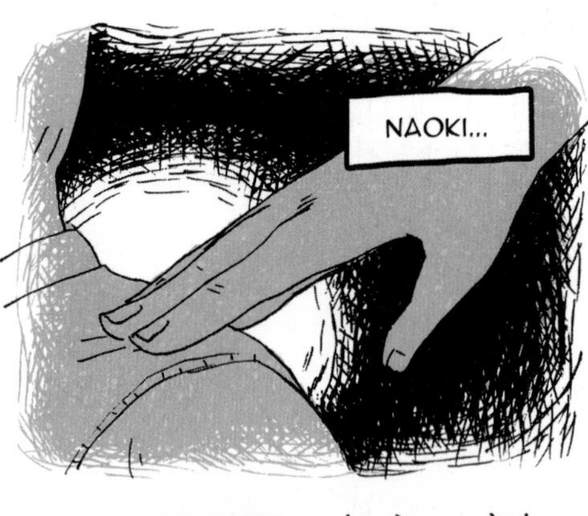
NAOKI...

DID SOMETHING HAPPEN...?

HM?
WHAT ARE YOU TALKING ABOUT?
WHAT ARE *YOU* TALKING ABOUT, HONEY?
HAHA.

LET'S HANG OUT AGAIN!

BYE GUYS!

OH!
JUST A MINUTE!

YOU FORGOT SOMETHING.

HAHA!

5. salieri

WE'RE VERY SORRY, KEN.
THAT'S OK, YUME.
I'LL FIGURE SOME-THING OUT.
DAMN IT.
ANOTHER STORY REJECTED.
GUESS I'D BETTER GO FIND SOME IDEAS.
HM...

THE WAY I CREATE HASN'T CHANGED MUCH SINCE I WAS A KID.

SOMETIMES IT DOESN'T WORK...
...BUT SOMETIMES, IT DOES.

I CONNECT THE THINGS IN FRONT OF ME...

AND START FORMING SOMETHING.

I RIDE
AROUND THE
NEIGHBORHOOD,
LOOKING
FOR IDEAS.

I CONSIDER BOTH
BLOCKS AND IDEAS
PHYSICAL OBJECTS.

WHEN I
CONNECT THE
THINGS I SEE,
I CAN BUILD
A STORY.

THIS TIME,
IT'LL BE A
MASTERPIECE!

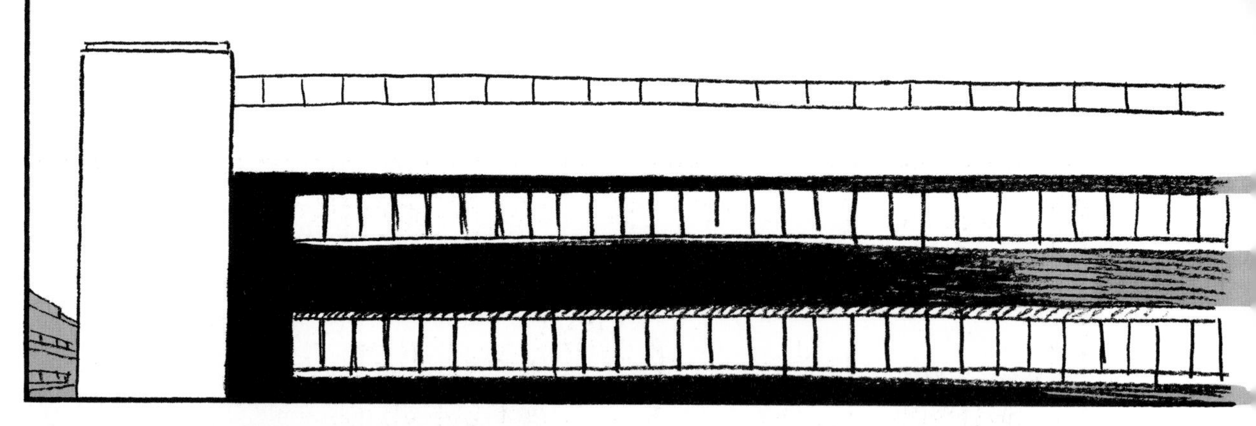

UM, ISN'T IT THE SAME PREMISE AS "THE BALLAD OF NARAYAMA?"

THIS IS ACTUALLY INTERESTING...
...BUT...

WHO SINGS IT?
I LOVE BALLADS!
THIS IS HOPELESS...

KEN, ARE YOU LISTENING?

TALK ABOUT BAD LUCK, HAVING THE SAME CONCEPT AS AN OLD MOVIE.
...

...OH MAN. HAHA!

BUT DON'T GIVE UP!

Y... YEAH!
NOW'S THE TIME!

YUME, IT'S READY!
I HAVE ANOTHER MASTERPIECE FOR YOU!

UH... HAVE YOU HEARD OF "DON QUIXOTE?"
THE NOVEL, "DON QUIXOTE."
FINISHED!

LET'S SEE...

THIS IS OUT OF THE QUESTION!!
AAAAAHH!!!

JUST BECAUSE THAT JERK CERVANTES WROTE THE SAME THING BEFORE ME...
HAHA!

GODDAMMIT!
THIS SUCKS!

...

THAT JUST MEANS YOU'VE BEEN BLESSED BY THE GODDESS OF CREATIVITY.
SHOULDN'T YOU JUST FIND A WAY TO HARNESS THAT?

GODDESS OF CREATIVITY!

THIS GUY AGAIN...
PLEASE SHOW ME THE WAY TO A MASTERPIECE ONLY I CAN MAKE!
SHUT UP AND GET LOST.

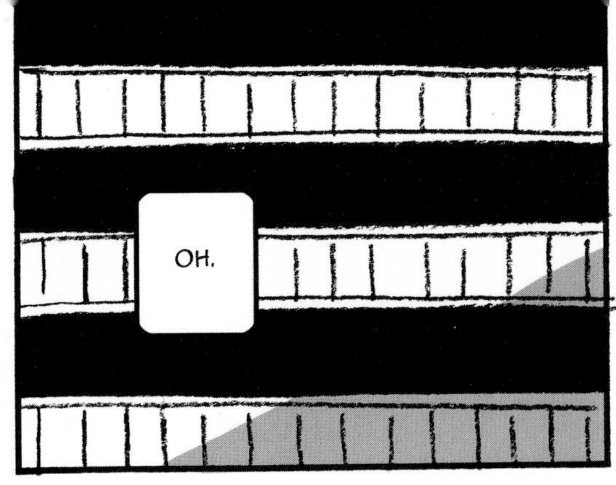
OH.

CONGRATULATIONS.
PHEW...

THIS IS ORIGINAL AND INTERESTING.
I ♥ Dad

YESSS!!

CLAP CLAP CLAP
I'M LOOKING FORWARD TO THE FINAL PRODUCT.
YES, SIR.

THANK YOU, GODDESS.

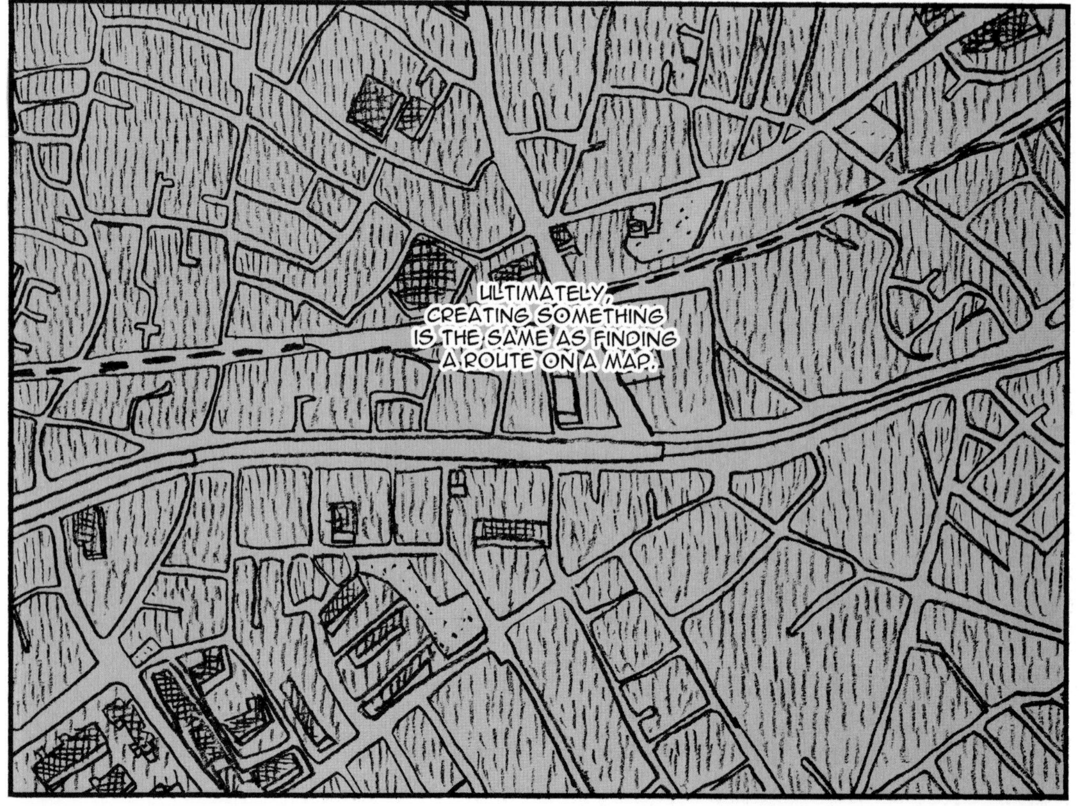
ULTIMATELY, CREATING SOMETHING IS THE SAME AS FINDING A ROUTE ON A MAP.

YOU LOOK FOR NEW POSSIBILITIES DOWN KNOWN STREETS...
I THINK I'LL GO THIS WAY.

WHAT A GREAT BOOKSTORE.

UN REGARD MODERNE
...AND DISCOVER THINGS YOU NEVER NOTICED BEFORE.

AND ANOTHER REWARD OF CREATION...
HEY MAN.
HEY.

I FOUND THIS AWESOME SHOP.

WANNA GRAB A DRINK?
RUNNING INTO PEOPLE ALONG THE WAY, AND GOING PART OF THE DISTANCE WITH THEM.

WHAT A DAY...
WOW... KEN IS REALLY OUT OF LUCK THIS MONTH...
めいさく
THIS LOOKS EXCITING.
RRRIN
ピリリ
IT'S YUME!
I WONDER WHAT'S UP.
MAYBE HE JUST WANTS TO REITER-ATE: "KEN, YOU'RE A GENIUS!" HAHA!

6. watermelon in summer

ミーン
SCREEE...
ミーン
SCREEE...
ミーン
SCREE...

ミーン
SCREE...
ミーン
SCREEE...

COUGH!
COUGH!

COUGH!

COUGH!

COUGH!
COUGH!

FOOD'S READY!

BEST COOK

OH!
DAMMIT...

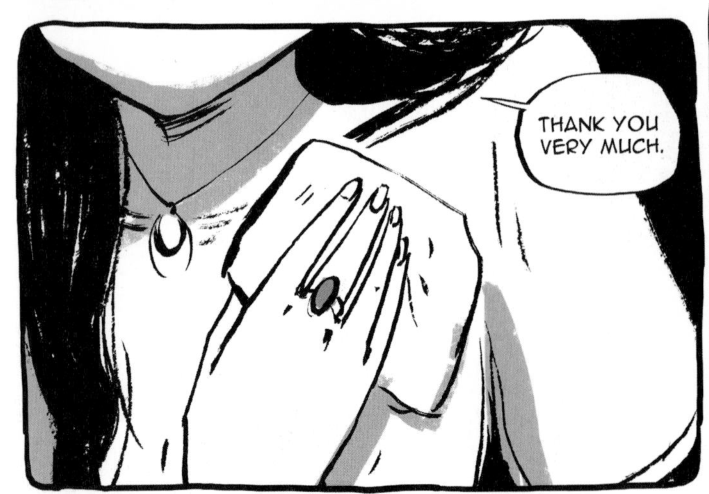
THANK YOU VERY MUCH.

THERE ARE STILL SOME SAUSAGES LEFT.
WOULD YOU LIKE ME TO COOK YOU SOMETHING ELSE?

SLIP
バタン
CLANK

GIVE ME A BREAK!

OH... UM... MAYBE I SHOULD GO GET THE WATERMELON.

LET'S PACK THIS UP.

HELLO.

SORRY TO BOTHER YOU ON YOUR FAMILY PICNIC, BUT...

I UH... I RAN OUT OF DRINKING WATER...
HAVE YOU GOT ANY TO SPARE?

OH MY GOD...

WHILE YOU'RE UP, MIKI HONEY, CAN YOU GRAB THAT BOTTLE FROM THE CAR?
EH?

I SEE...
HERE YOU GO.

SO...
DO YOU LIVE CLOSE BY?

NO, MY WORD, NOT AT ALL.
YEAH, THAT'S IT, DUDE.

ポン
BUMP
YOU CAN TAKE THE WHOLE BOTTLE.

TH... THANK YOU.
WELL... I'LL BE ON MY WAY THEN...

I'M SAYING THERE WAS NO REASON FOR US TO HAVE THIS DAMN PICNIC!
HERE WE GO AGAIN.

I WAS A BIT AFRAID OF MEETING PEOPLE ONLINE...

YOU AND ME BOTH MA'AM. BUT I THINK WE GOT OURSELVES A NICE GROUP TODAY.

BEFORE LEAVING THIS WORLD.

BUT... I JUST WANTED TO HAVE A NICE MEAL.

WHATEVER.

THAT SHOULD DO IT.

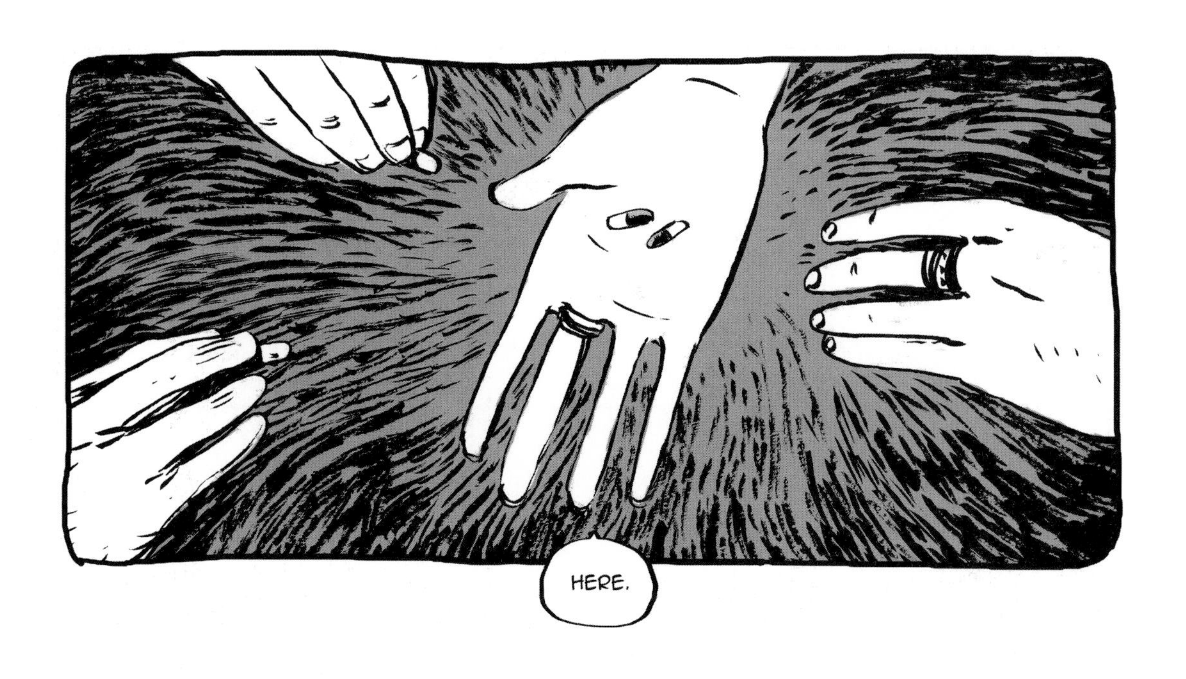
HERE.

HEY!

YOU PEOPLE!
WHAT THE HELL DO YOU THINK YOU'RE DOING!

YOU IDIOTS...

YOU CALL THAT FIRE EXTINGUI-SHED?!

YOU WANT TO SET THE WHOLE FOREST ON FIRE?

OH, NOT TO WORRY, SIR.
WE WERE JUST ABOUT TO PUT IT OUT.

AND WHAT IS ALL THIS TRASH?!

HAHA...
OH DEAR, WE'D COMPLETELY FORGOTTEN!

YOU WERE GOING TO LEAVE ALL THIS BEHIND!

AND THAT CAR OF YOURS...
PLEASE! GIVE ME A BREAK!

LEAVE US ALONE!
SHOVE
YOU'RE INTERFERING!
WHAT?
WE WERE JUST GOING TO...

THUNK
THUD
DON'T YOU TALK BACK TO ME!

WHERE ARE YOU GOING?
OW...

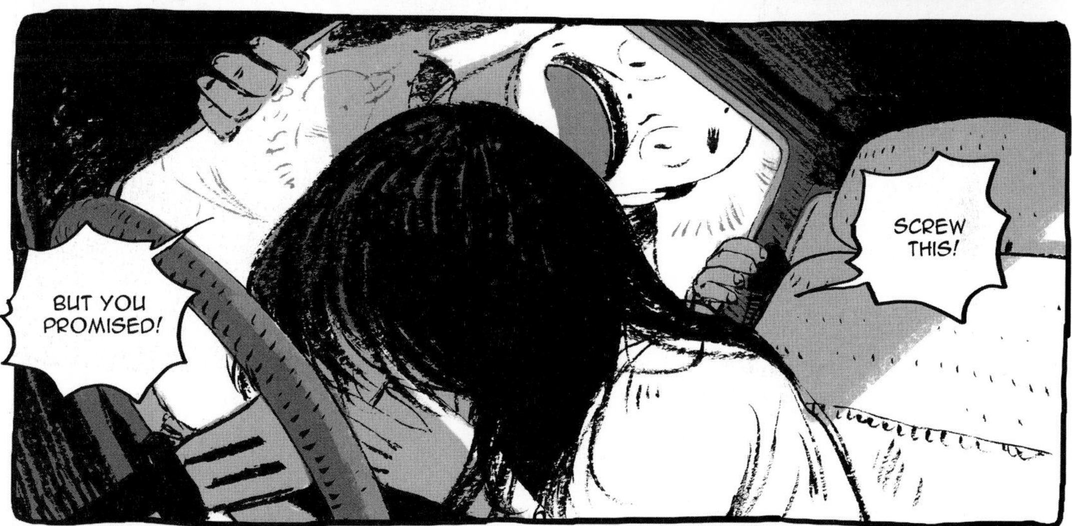
BUT YOU PROMISED!
SCREW THIS!

ME TOO!
LET ME IN TOO, MAN!
PLEASE WAIT!

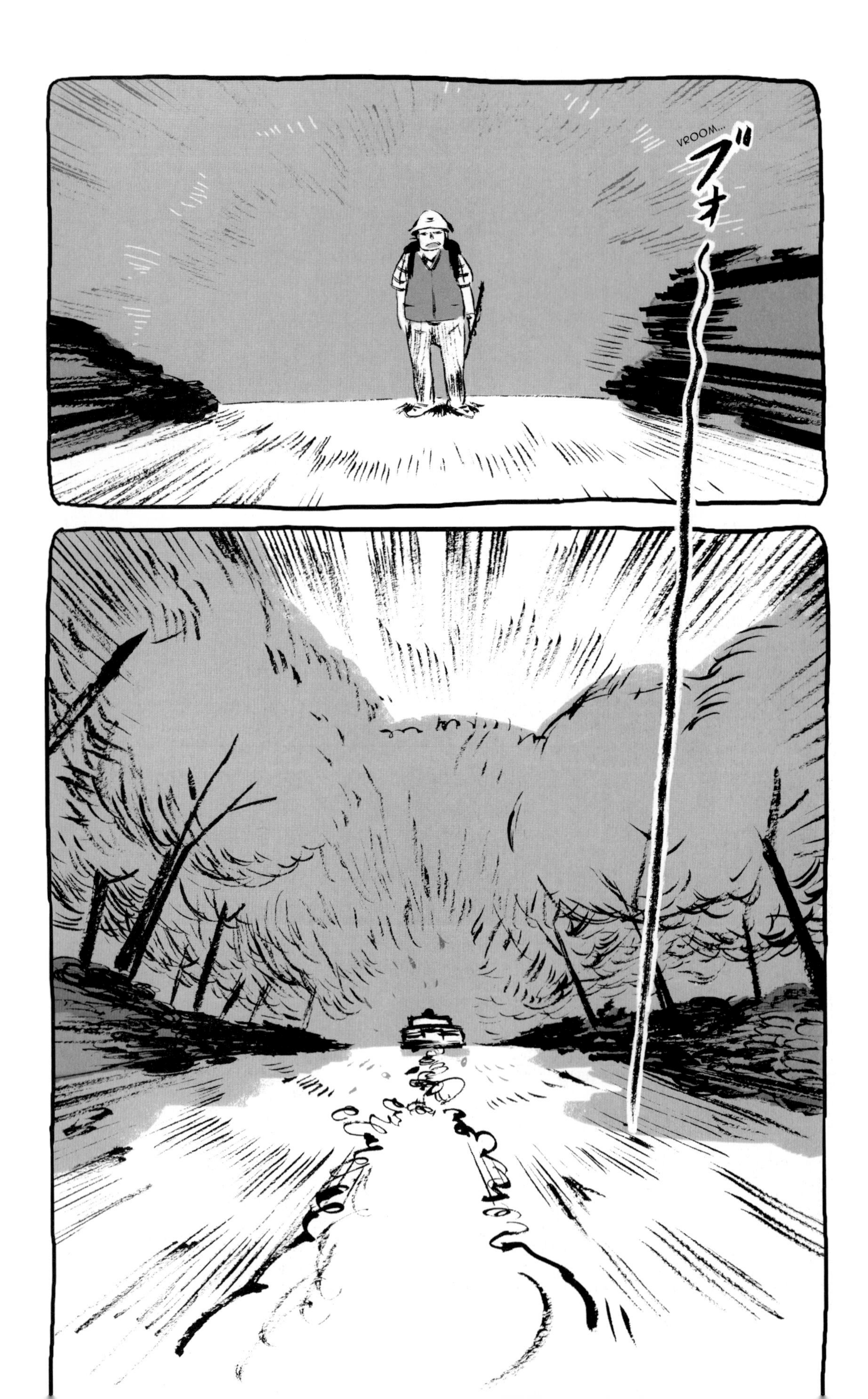
VROOM...
ブオ〜〜

UM... WHERE TO?

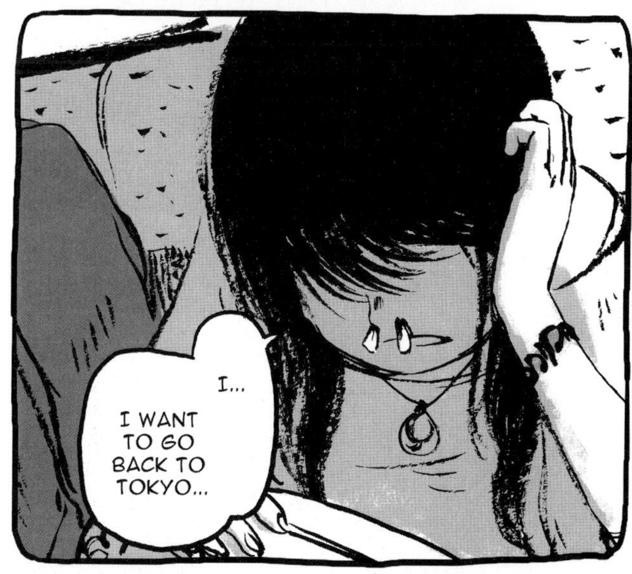
I... I WANT TO GO BACK TO TOKYO...

OH!

WE FORGOT THE WATERMELON...
VROOM...
ブオ〜

BEAUTIFUL NATURE...
CLEAN AIR...

I UNDERSTAND WHY CITY FOLK WOULD WANT TO COME HERE.
BUT WHO DID THOSE DISRUPTIVE PEOPLE THINK THEY WERE.

IN THE END, ONE'S FINAL MOMENTS...

SCREEE...
SCREEE...

...SHOULD BE
SPENT ALONE.

SCREEE...
SCREEE...
SCREEE...

7. merci

QU'EST-CE QUE VOUS AVEZ DIT TOUT À L'HEURE?
'AI RIEN 'RIS DU OUT.

CASSEZ-VOUS D'ICI.
HOW DO YOU SAY "HAMMER" IN FRENCH...

UH... WHAT DID HE JUST SAY?

OH! I REMEMBER!
EUH...

UGH...
チョキ
SNAP
チョキ
SNAP
チョキ
SNAP

チョキ
SNAP
チョキ
SNAP

WHAT IS THIS ODD FEELING...

I HATE THAT
I CAN'T EXPRESS
MYSELF IN WORDS.

514-H
le film
MAC MAHON

I FEEL LIKE
I'M SURROUNDED
BY WALLS MADE
OF AIR.
VINAIGRE

HAMMER
OK. WHAT WOULD ALAIN DELON DO?

caillerie
4

HE WOULD SAY, "ANYTHING TO GET THE MESSAGE ACROSS."

THIS IS IT.
ちりりん
RING RING!

QU'EST-CE QUE JE PEUX FAIRE POUR VOUS?
I WOULD LIKE A HAMMER.
UN HAMMER.
TAP,
TAP,
ALMOND,
TAP!
BANG,
OUCH!
AH!
UN HAMMER, S'IL VOUS PLAIT.

AH AH AH AH AH AH AH

AH AH AH AH

AH AH AH AH AH AH AH AH AH AH AH AH AH AH

I DID IT!

ME... MERCI.
DE RIEN, QUOI.

ALLEZ, TIENS TON MACHIN.

SHE UNDERSTOOD ME! I WAS ABLE TO COMMUNICATE!

SHE LAUGHED AT ME, BUT...
I'M AMAZING!

WHAT A WONDERFUL FEELING!

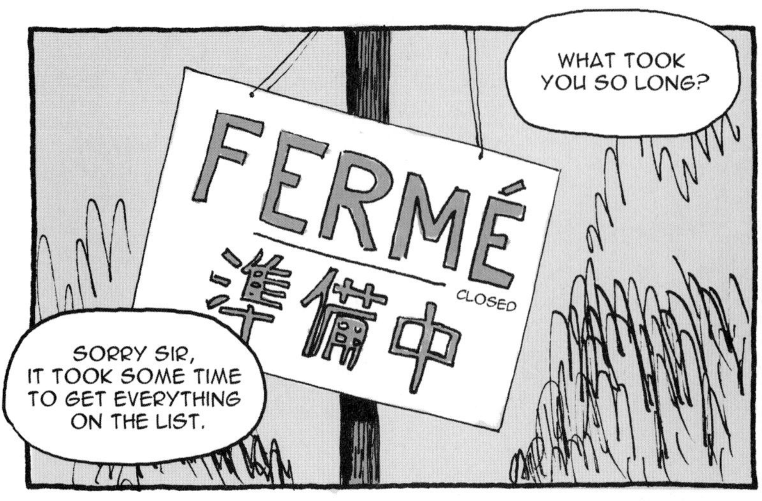
WHAT TOOK YOU SO LONG?
FERMÉ
準備中
CLOSED
SORRY SIR, IT TOOK SOME TIME TO GET EVERYTHING ON THE LIST.

THIS HELPS.
PLEASE UNPACK THAT BOX AND STOCK THE SHELVES.
YES, SIR.

HM? WHY THE TONGS?
A LITTLE SOMETHING EXTRA. HAHA.
AH WELL.
I'M SURE THEY'LL COME IN HANDY.

COMPADRE, YO ME VOY A IR YENDO YA...

¡¿QUÉ PRETENDE HACER CON ESE MARTILLO?!

TUMBLE
¡NO, NO, POR FAVOR!

QUE YO LE JURO QUE LE DEVUELVO HASTA EL ÚLTIMO FRANCO MAÑANA MISMO.

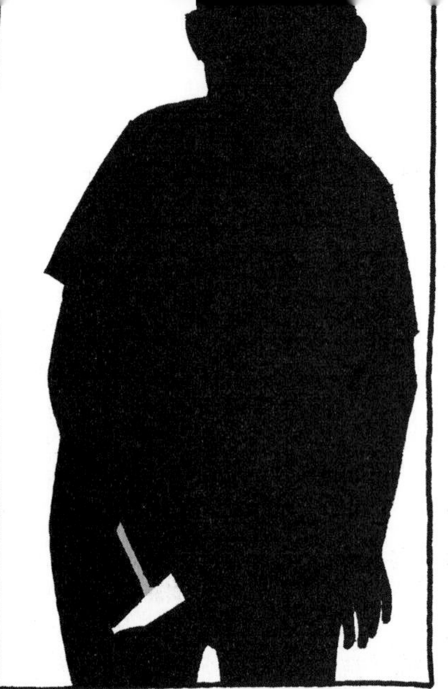

POR LA GLORIA DE MI MADRE.
I SAID SHUT UP!
ENOUGH WITH YOUR LAME EXCUSES.
THUNK
BESIDES, I DON'T UNDERSTAND A DAMN WORD YOU'RE SAYING.

バタン
SLAM!
SHIT.

8. lying is bad

WHAT THE DEVIL...
THANKS FOR WAITING, CHIEF INSPECTOR.

KANTA. ANYONE INJURED?
IT'S A MIRACLE, SIR. EVERYONE IS OK, WITH JUST A FEW SCRAPES.
GOOD!

THEY'RE ALL IN A BIT OF SHOCK, AND NO ONE IS TALK-ING.
THIS IS WHAT WE KNOW SO FAR:

DID YOU FIND OUT WHAT ACTUALLY HAPPENED?
WELL...

ABOUT AN HOUR AGO, A CUSTOMER ENTERED THE SHOP...

...AND ORDERED A SET MEAL.

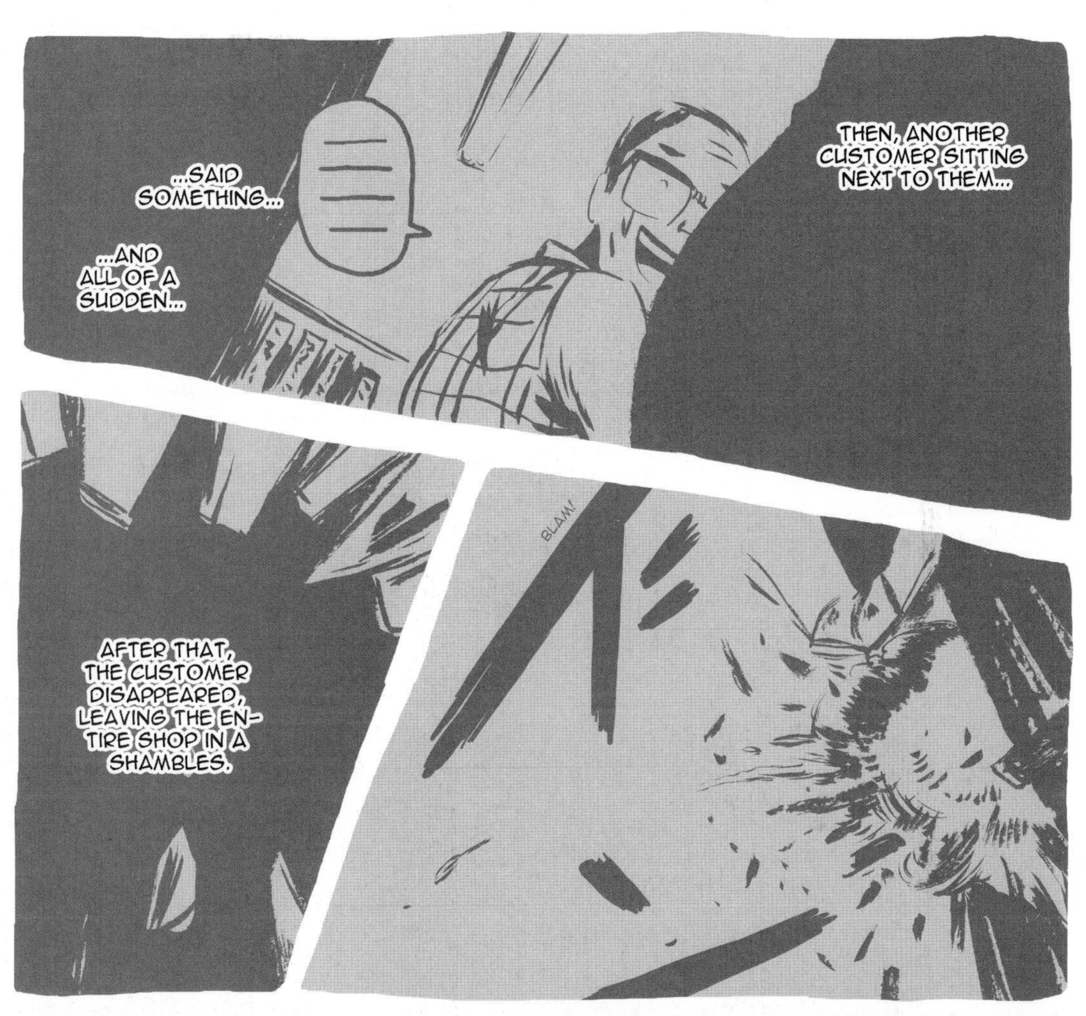
THEN, ANOTHER CUSTOMER SITTING NEXT TO THEM...
...SAID SOMETHING...
...AND ALL OF A SUDDEN...
BLAM!
AFTER THAT, THE CUSTOMER DISAPPEARED, LEAVING THE EN- TIRE SHOP IN A SHAMBLES.

I SEE.
DO YOU KNOW WHAT WAS SAID?
UNFORTUNATELY...
UM, EXCUSE ME.

WE'VE FOUND ANOTHER SURVIVOR IN THE RUBBLE.

WHAT HAPPENED IN THERE?

SORRY TO ASK AT A TIME LIKE THIS, BUT...
WOULD YOU MIND ANSWERING A FEW QUES-TIONS?

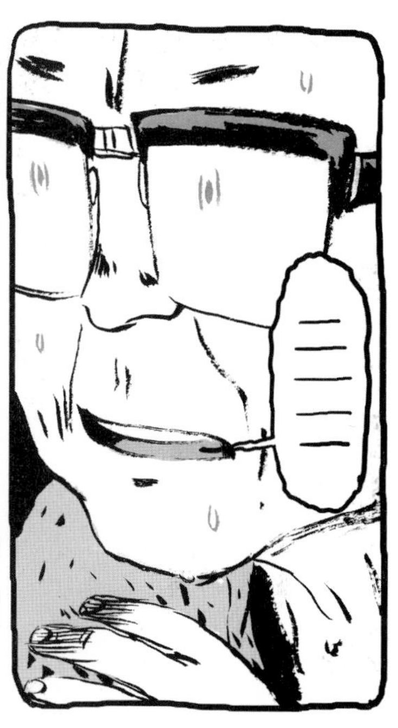

"YOU CAN EVEN EAT BEEF BOWL..."

I THINK I KNOW WHO IS RESPONSIBLE FOR THIS.

"EVEN... BEEF BOWL..."

WHAT ELSE HAPPENED?
SAY SOME-THING!
PLEASE STOP, HE'S IN-JURED!

LET ME GET BACK TO YOU, SIR...
...WE'VE GOT TO STOP THIS.

KANTA. ARE YOU SERIOUS?

I HAVE A HUNCH...

WHAT DO YOU MEAN BY THAT, KANTA?
THESE ARE THE PEOPLE WHO WERE AROUND AT THE TIME OF THE INCIDENT.

...YOU'RE VERY GOOD AT USING CHOPSTICKS.

BACK OFF ALREADY!
IT'S OK.

HE'S NO LONGER A SUSPECT.
YOU CAN LET HIM GO.
HUH?

HOW VERY JAPANESE OF ALL OF YOU.
ARE YOU MAKING FUN OF US? UM...

CLANG

WELL THEN...
ISN'T IT GREAT THAT JAPAN HAS FOUR SEASONS?

ARE YOU OK, MISS?

...
THANK YOU, YES.

UM, THANKS...
CAN I GO NOW?

SO.

I'M SORRY! I'M VEGE-TARIAN!
OH... I APOLOGIZE FOR THE INCONVE-NIENCE...
SNIFFLE!

THAT LEAVES...

SOMEBODY CALL A DOCTOR!
HEY! ARE YOU OK?!
UGH.
HURRY!
ウォオオオッ
GRRR...

UNH.
AH!

ウオオオオオオオッ
GRRR...
MY GOD...
I KNEW IT.

PLEASE TRY AND IMAGINE WHAT IT WAS LIKE FOR THIS PERSON WHEN THEY FIRST ARRIVED IN JAPAN.
WHAT DOES THIS MEAN?
...
YOU MAY FIND IT DIFFICULT TO UNDERSTAND, BUT...

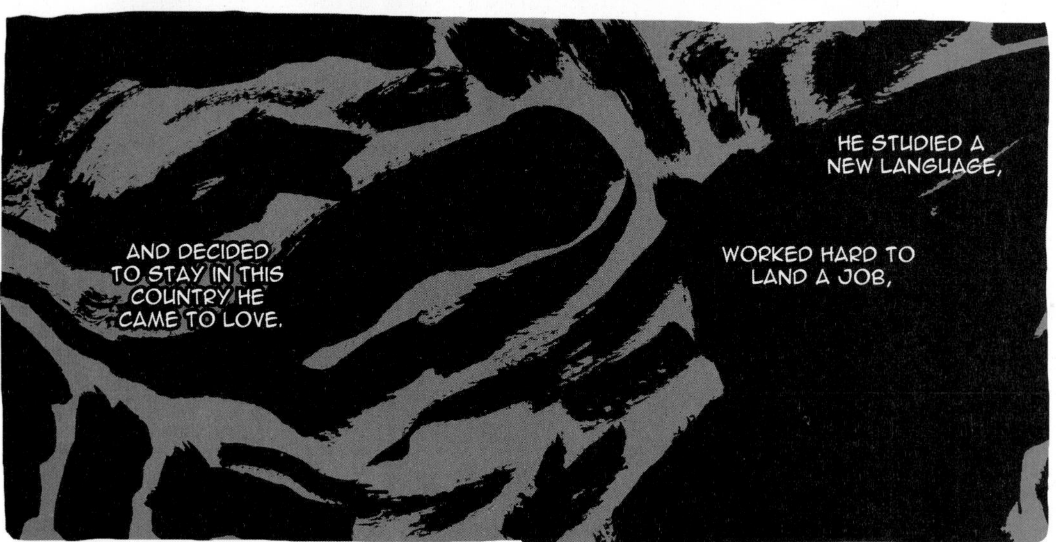
HE STUDIED A NEW LANGUAGE,
WORKED HARD TO LAND A JOB,
AND DECIDED TO STAY IN THIS COUNTRY HE CAME TO LOVE.

BUT NO MATTER HOW HARD HE TRIES, HE'S ALWAYS CONSIDERED A "FOREIGNER."
EVEN AFTER 10, 20 YEARS, HE'S ONLY EVER TREATED AS AN OUTSIDER.
THOSE HURTFUL MEMORIES, ALONG WITH ALL THE SADNESS AND LONELINESS...

... GIVE WAY TO FEEL- INGS OF ANGER.
IN CONCLUSION, THE ENTITY THAT GAVE RISE TO THIS MONSTER...

IS THIS SOCIETY AS A WHOLE.
WHAT IS HE GOING TO DO...
IF HE CARRIES ON LIKE THIS, WE'LL HAVE NO CHOICE BUT TO TAKE HIM DOWN!
IT'S ALRIGHT. JUST WATCH ME.

ズ
SLUMP
LISTEN UP! YOUR JAPANESE IS TERRIBLE!
THE WAY YOU YAMMER ON THE SUBWAY WITH YOUR FRIENDS IS REALLY ANNOYING!
IT IRRITATES EVERYONE AROUND YOU!
AND...
THE THING JAPANESE ALWAYS SAY, ABOUT YOU LOOKING LIKE A HOLLYWOOD ACTOR...
ズ
SLUMP
ウォォォォ
GRRR

OF COURSE IT'S A TOTAL LIE!!
GRRR
ウォォォォォォォォッ

IS IT GONE?

...HE'S PROBABLY RETURNED TO HIS NATIVE COUNTRY.
HIS ANGER MUST'VE REACHED ITS THRESHOLD...
HOW COULD SUCH AN AWFUL THING HAPPEN?

I THINK I'LL TRY TALKING NORMALLY NEXT TIME.

I GUESS IF WE TALK TO THEM OUT OF KINDNESS, THEY INTERPRET IT A DIFFE-RENT WAY...
MAYBE YOU'RE RIGHT.

YEAH!
THERE'S GOT TO BE A WAY FOR US TO GET ALONG!

KANTA, HOW DID YOU FIGURE ALL THIS OUT?

WHAT A WONDERFUL COUNTRY THIS IS...

WELL,
MY MOTHER IS FROM ANOTHER COUNTRY.

I UNDERSTAND HIS FEELINGS VERY WELL.

BY THE WAY...
YOUR... JAPANESE IS REALLY GOOD!

OH...

式場入口
*CEREMONIAL HALL

OH, IT'S SO NICE TO SEE YOU!

YOU'VE GROWN INTO A BEAUTIFUL WOMAN.
YOU TOO, MA'AM.
HEE HEE!

DID YOU COME HERE ALONE?
YOU AREN'T GETTING ANY YOUNGER, DEAR, WHY DON'T YOU GET MARRIED?
BOOM

9. par-tay

うお、
うお、
うお、
OTYA

RED WINE
TEA
BREAD
WELL...
OLIVES
CHICK PEA STEW
PROSCIUTTO

LET'S EAT!!

CHOMP
CHOMP

AAH...

もぐもぐもぐもぐ
GOBBLE GOBBLE
ぐもぐ
もぐも
もぐもぐもぐもぐ
HOURS BEFORE...
ピンポーン♪
DING DONG
Hrm
Hrm
ピンポ〜ン
DING DONG
HUH?

WHAT'S WITH THE SLEEPY FACE?
TAKING ANOTHER NAP?

SHUT UP. IT'S BECAUSE I WAS WORKING. WORKING!
WHAT ARE THESE GUYS DOING HERE...

I'M EXCITED WE FINALLY GET TO TRY "KEN'S SIGNATURE DISH."
HERE'S THE WINE WE PROMISED.

"KEN'S SIGNATURE DISH"
WAIN
I'D COMPLETELY FORGOTTEN...

REALLY?
AWW. SO CUTE!
LOOKS LIKE A CAT'S BEEN SHITTING IN YOUR FLOWER POTS AGAIN.
HEY LOOK, A SUPER NES.
YOU GET TO DO THE ANNOYING PART.
O WASH YOUR HANDS.
SO, WHAT CAN I DO?

MY FRIDGE IS EMPTY.
I FORGOT TO GET GROCERIES!!
GUESS I'LL HAVE TO MAKE SOMETHING OUT OF NOTHING...*
CAN
MILK
BEANS
BEANS
CEREALS
* NIGHTMARE: "WHAT GIVES? YOU WERE SO CONFIDENT BACK IN CHAPTER 5."

YOU'RE IN CHARGE OF THE POTATOES. CUT THEM INTO SMALL PIECES.
WHAT ABOUT ME?

ANYWAYS...

LEAVE IT TO US!
BUT SHOW US HOW YOU DO IT.

HERE. TAKE THIS.

I'M OUT OF IDEAS!!
YOU'RE A COMIC ARTIST! MAKE UP A STORY AND CREATE SOME ATMOSPHERE...
I WILL NEVER REVEAL TO YOU MY SECRET RECIPE.

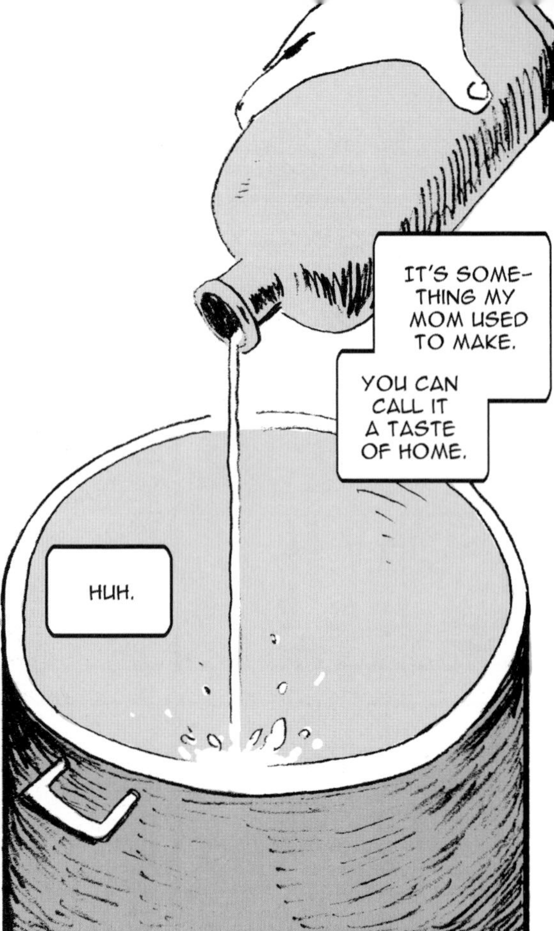
IT'S SOME-
THING MY
MOM USED
TO MAKE.
YOU CAN
CALL IT
A TASTE
OF HOME.
HUH.

SHE
ALWAYS SAYS
"CUISINE BEGINS
WITH A GOOD
SOUP STOCK."
DIDN'T SHE...?

WITH A GOOD
SOUP STOCK, THE
INGREDIENTS
ARE ELEVATED TO
THE NEXT LEVEL.

AND
THEN
I ADD
WATER.
しゅわ～～
SHHH

POTATOES
PLEASE.

TIME FOR MY SECRET SEASONING.

NO PEEKING.

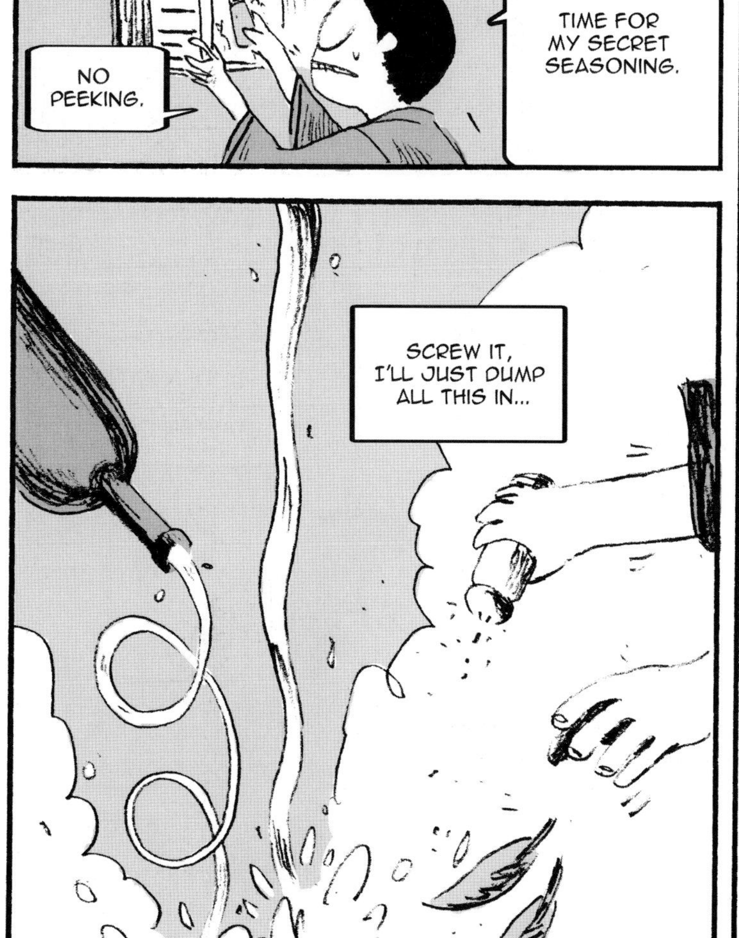

THEN I LET IT STEW FOR A BIT.
WE'LL BE PLAYING VIDEO GAMES!
RUN RUN
YAY!

FSSS

GOD, PLEASE MAKE THIS ACTUALLY TASTE GOOD...

BRING IT ON!
YOU'RE NOT READY!

MEANWHILE...

AND THEN...

JERK.
YOU'RE GETTING ON MY NERVES.
YOU WIN
I WIN!

IT'S TRANS-FORMED INTO A CURRY...
WELL, WHATEVER.

SNIFF, SNIFF.

LET'S EAT!
YAY!

PLEASE, GOD...

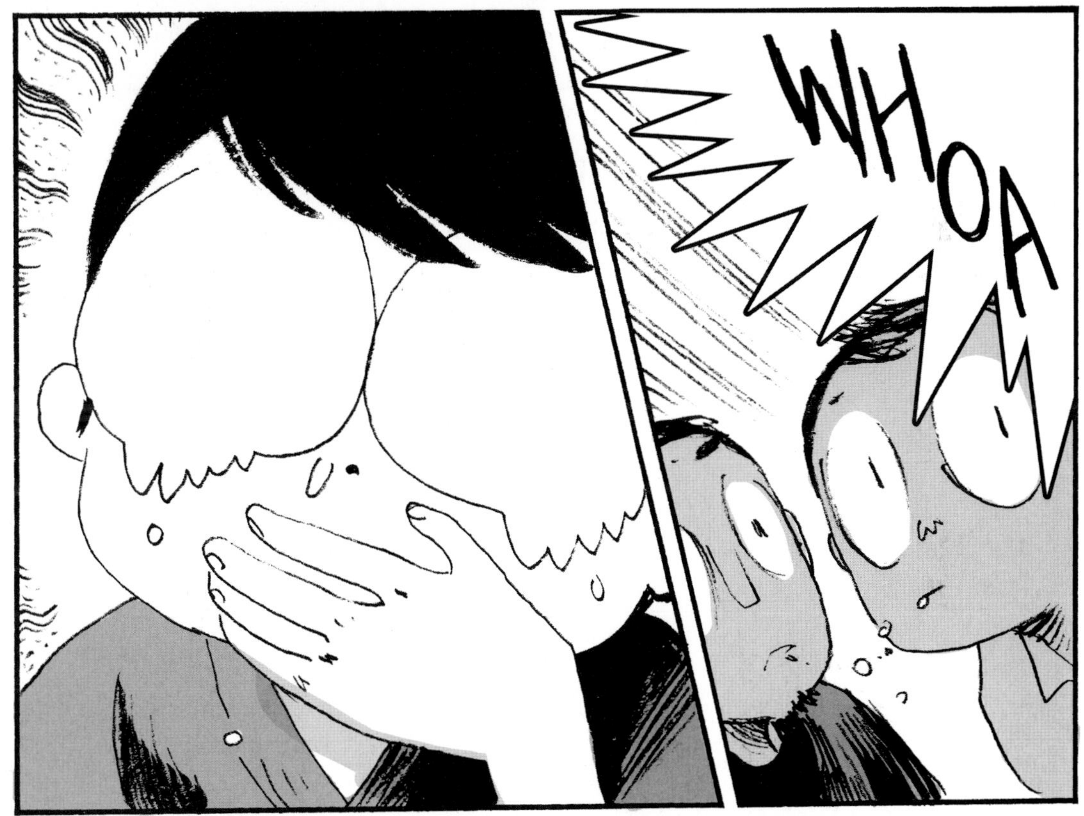
WHOA

I JUST MIGHT BE A GENIUS!!
THIS IS AMAZING!

YOU CAN TASTE EACH INGREDIENT.
AND THEY'RE ALL PERFECTLY BALANCED.

IT'S REALLY DELICIOUS!

WHAT AN UNUSUAL TEXTURE!
WHAT A SWEET AFTERTASTE!
AND SO FULL OF *UMAMI!*

THEY SAY THE WORLD'S MOST DELICIOUS COFFEE IS MADE WITH BEANS EXTRACTED FROM THE DROPPINGS OF THE CIVET CAT.

AND TOP QUALITY PERFUMES CONTAIN GREY AMBER, WHICH COMES FROM WHALE INTESTINES.

THERE ARE ALL KINDS OF OUTRA-GEOUS THINGS IN THIS WORLD...

BUT IF YOU CAN MAKE THEM WORK TO YOUR ADVANTAGE...
...SOMETHING BEAUTIFUL WILL COME OF IT.
...MAYBE.

GOOD OL' FASHIONED CHICK PEAS & CHORIZO OF YORE

INGREDIENTS

- 400G CHICK PEAS (DRIED OR CANNED)
- 200G CHORIZO SAUSAGE
  (OR 200G BEEF + PAPRIKA POWDER TO TASTE)
- 1X LARGE POTATO
- 1X SMALL ONION
- 1X CARROT
- 1X BAY LEAF
- A DASH OF WHITE WINE
- OLIVE OIL, TO TASTE
- SALT & PEPPER, TO TASTE

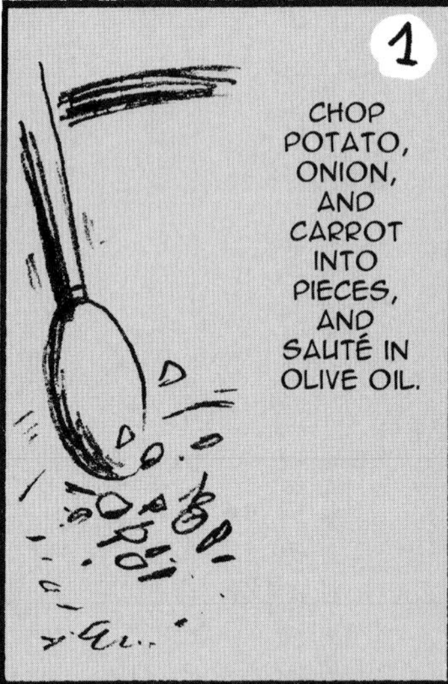

BON APPÉTIT!!

10. the victory sign

パキッ
CRACK!

THERE YOU GO, KOSUKE!

KEITA...

CAN YOU STICK AROUND FOR A BIT LONGER?

WHAT ARE YOU SAYING?
I DON'T GIVE A SHIT ANY-MORE.
WHAT DO YOU WANNA DO?

WHY THE HELL WOULD SHE WANT A DIVORCE?
I JUST GOTTA SAY THIS... WOMEN ARE A PAIN IN THE ASS!

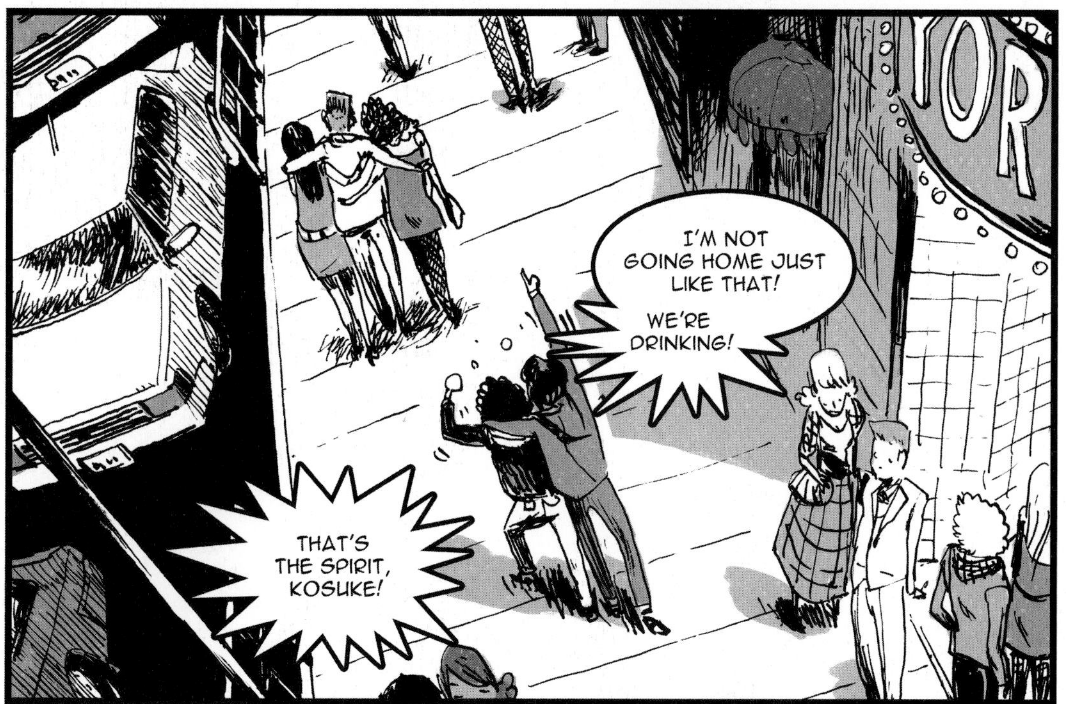
I'M NOT GOING HOME JUST LIKE THAT!
WE'RE DRINKING!
THAT'S THE SPIRIT, KOSUKE!

スナック
びなす
*VENUS SNACK BAR

I GUESS YOU'VE KNOWN EACH OTHER FOR YEARS.
HAHA!

WE WERE ON THE HIGH SCHOOL BASEBALL TEAM.

IT'S TRUE!!
KOSUKE IS THE PERSON I RESPECT THE MOST, EVEN TODAY. HE'S LIKE A BIG BROTHER TO ME.
QUIT IT, YOU'RE EMBARRA-SSING ME!

THIS GUY. THIS GUY RIGHT HERE. HE'S AMA-ZING.
OH STOP IT.

WHEN I WAS TEN, I MOVED WITH MY FAMILY TO A NEW TOWN.
I HAD NO FRIENDS, SO I WAS AIMLESSLY WANDERING ALL THE TIME.

SWISH!

SWISH!
SWISH!
THEN ONE DAY...

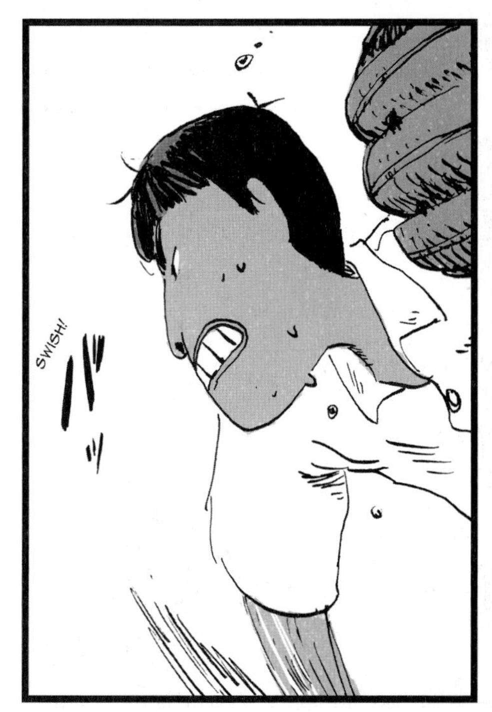
SWISH!

BONK!

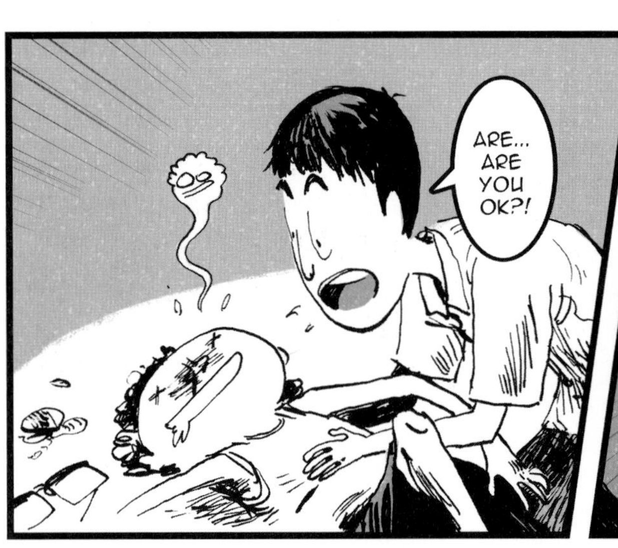
ARE... ARE YOU OK?!

WELL, SEE YOU TOMO-RROW.

I'D MADE MY FIRST FRIEND.

WE WENT TO THE SAME MIDDLE SCHOOL AND HIGH SCHOOL, AND JOINED THE SAME BASEBALL CLUB.

I NEED A LITTLE BREAK.
ARE YOU OK, KOSUKE?

IT'S BEEN YEARS SINCE WE STARTED BASEBALL.

I DON'T FEEL LIKE I'M IMPRO-VING.

EVEN SO...

NEXT WEEK'S GAME IS THE LAST ONE.
GUESS I'LL BE GRADUATING WITHOUT HITTING A SINGLE HOME RUN.

FEELS LIKE THERE'S NO POINT TO ANY OF THIS HARD WORK.

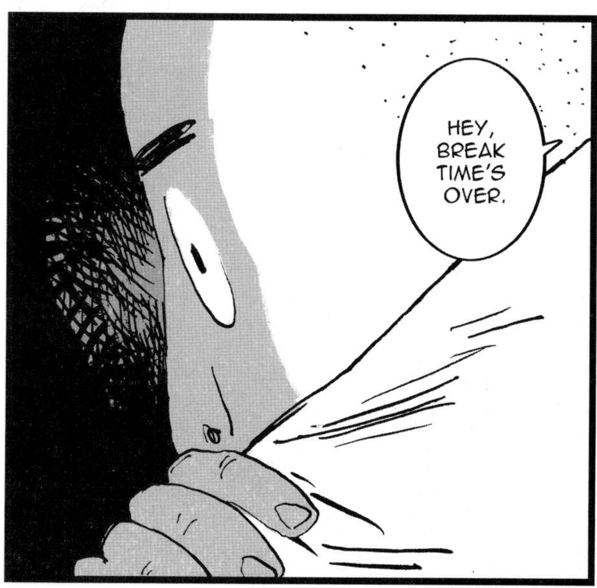
HEY, BREAK TIME'S OVER.

HERE.

パキッ
CRACK
GRAB THE BAT A BIT TIGHTER.
YEAH.
HERE GOES.

WOW!

KEITA...

THERE YOU GO, KOSUKE!

THE DAY OF THE GAME FINALLY ARRIVED.

WE WERE BEHIND BY ONE POINT...
THE LAST BATTER STEPPED UP TO THE PLATE.

IT WAS KOSUKE.

GOOOO
GOOOOOO

WE DON'T NEED ONE.

THIS IS NOT GOOD.
WHO'S THE PINCH HITTER, COACH?

GOOOOO
GOOOOO
GOOOOO

GOOOOOO
GOOOOOO

SWISH!

GO, KOSUKE, GO!!

ドドドド
BRRRRRM
HRM.

パキッ
CRACK!

KO... KOSUKE! ARE YOU ALRIGHT?
AARGH...

...

NO MATTER HOW HARD I WORKED BACK THEN, I'M STILL ON THE VERGE OF A DIVORCE!

IT'LL WORK OUT. YOU'RE YOU, AFTER ALL.

HERE.
PLEASE KEEP THE CHANGE.

COME ON, I'M TAKING YOU HOME.

GENTLEMEN...?

SO... WHAT HAPPENED AT THE GAME?

WELL THEN.

SLAM!

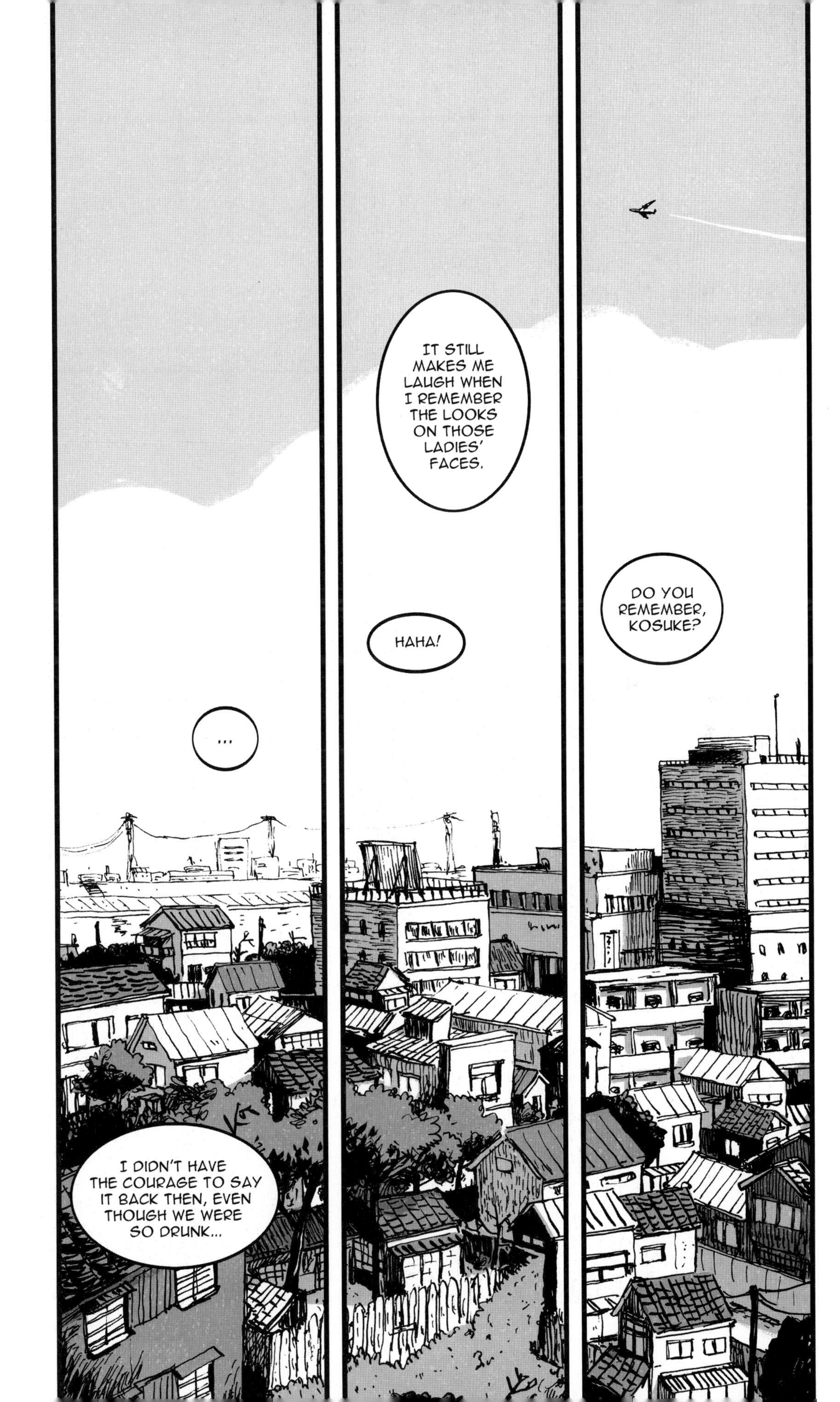
DO YOU REMEMBER, KOSUKE?
IT STILL MAKES ME LAUGH WHEN I REMEMBER THE LOOKS ON THOSE LADIES' FACES.
HAHA!
...
I DIDN'T HAVE THE COURAGE TO SAY IT BACK THEN, EVEN THOUGH WE WERE SO DRUNK...

BUT I ALWAYS ADMIRED YOU MOST WHEN I SAW YOU WORKING HARD.

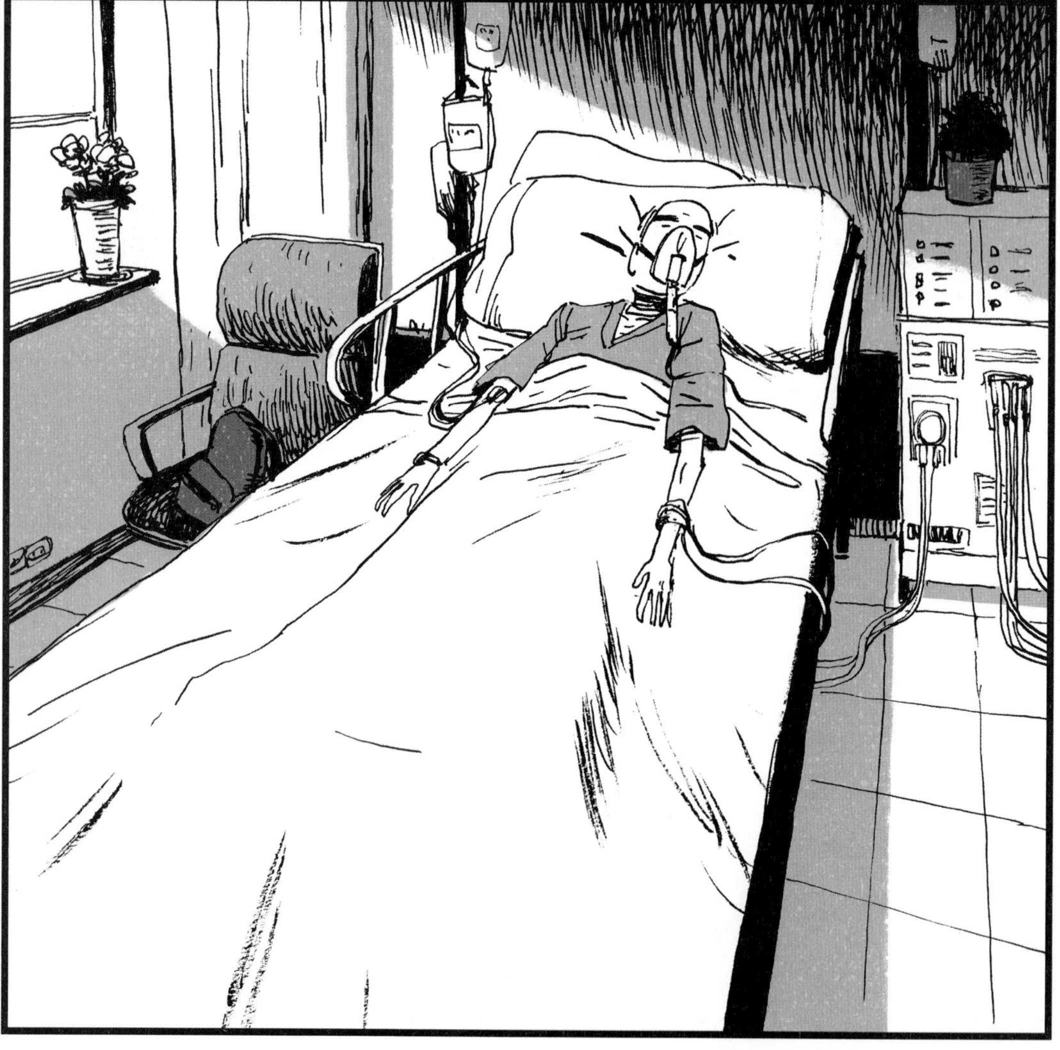

パキッ
CRACK!

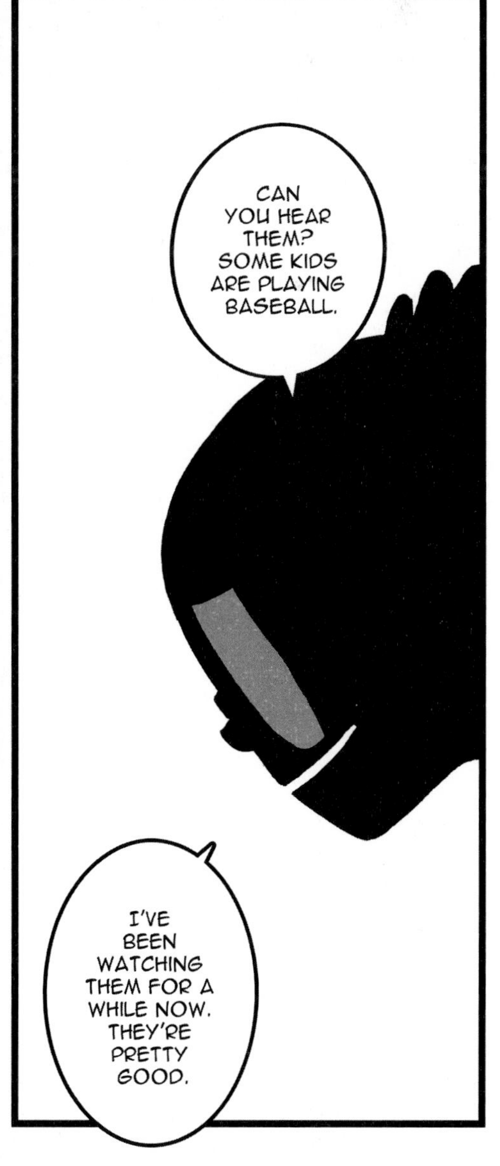
CAN YOU HEAR THEM? SOME KIDS ARE PLAYING BASEBALL.
I'VE BEEN WATCHING THEM FOR A WHILE NOW. THEY'RE PRETTY GOOD.

HOW BORING MY LIFE WOULD'VE BEEN IF I HADN'T MET YOU.

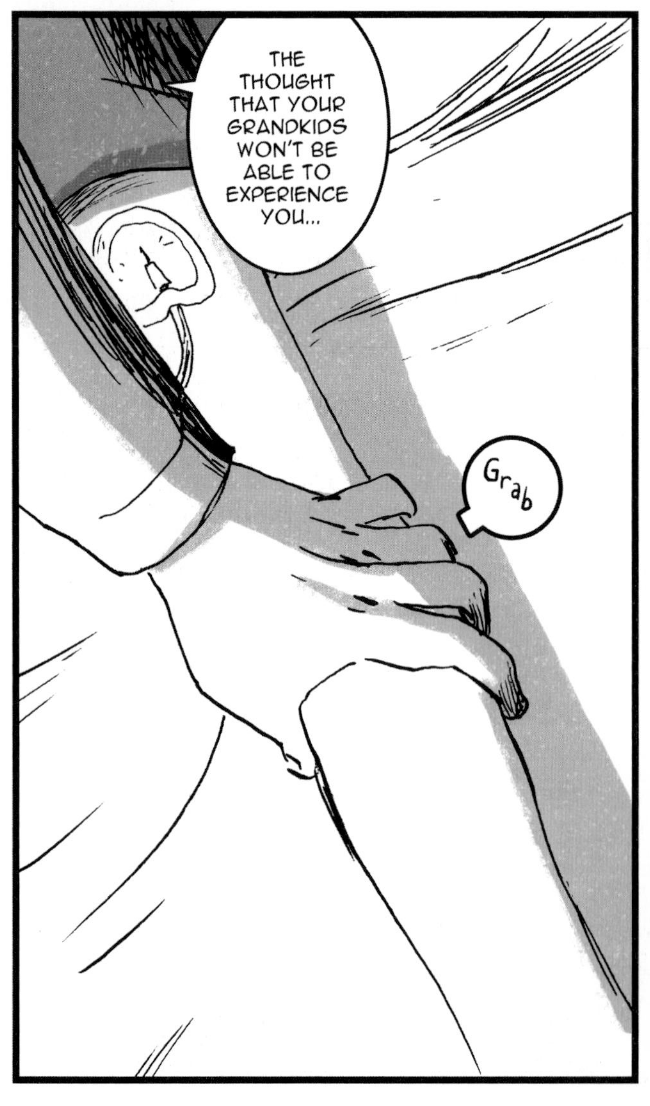
THE THOUGHT THAT YOUR GRANDKIDS WON'T BE ABLE TO EXPERIENCE YOU...
Grab

THAT'S WHY IT'S SO FRUS-TRATING.

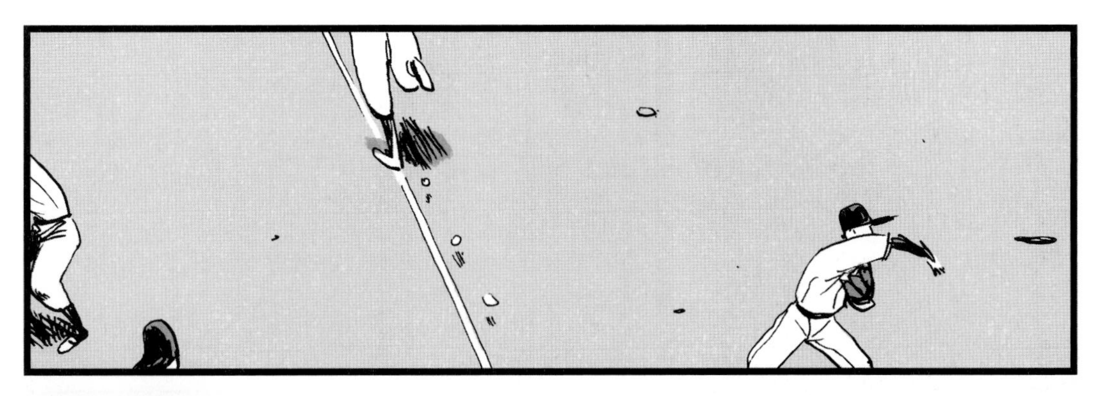

THIS WORLD IS SO UNFAIR.

HELLO MADAM.
YOU CAME AGAIN TODAY.

OH, HELLO! THANKS FOR ALL YOU DO.

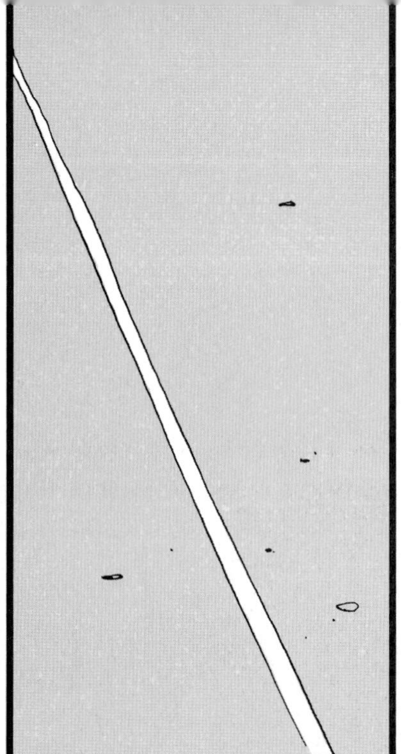

KOSUKE'S HAVING HIS OPERATION TOMORROW.

HORCH

THAT'S NOT LIKE YOU TO LOOK SO DOWN, KEITA.
OH?

KOSUKE ALWAYS SAID, EVER SINCE WE WERE YOUNG...

"IF I MANAGED TO LEAD A HAPPY LIFE..."
"...IT'S THANKS TO KEITA, WHO WAS ALWAYS THERE FOR ME."

パキッ
CRACK!

11. first snow

SHAVED ICE
氷

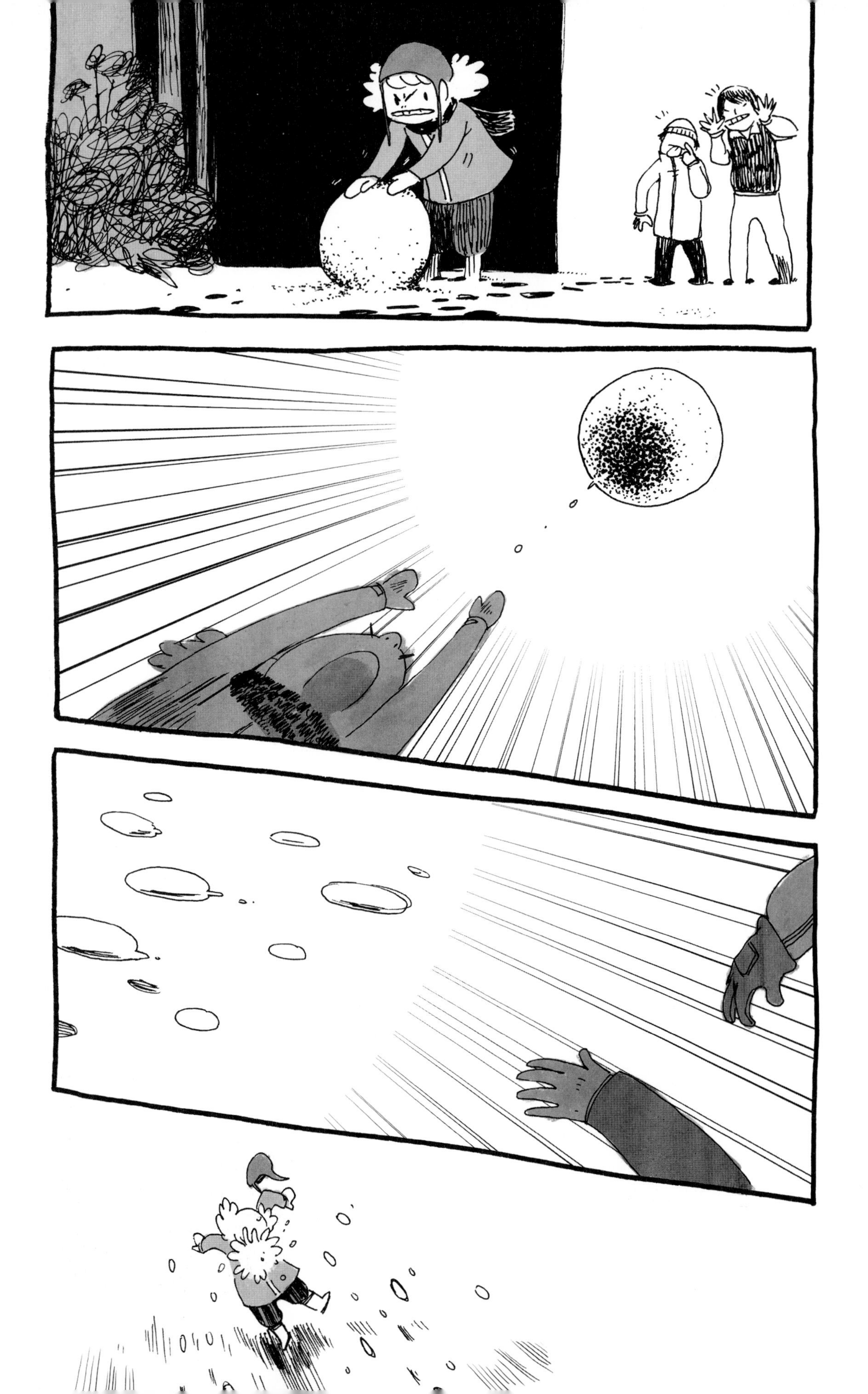

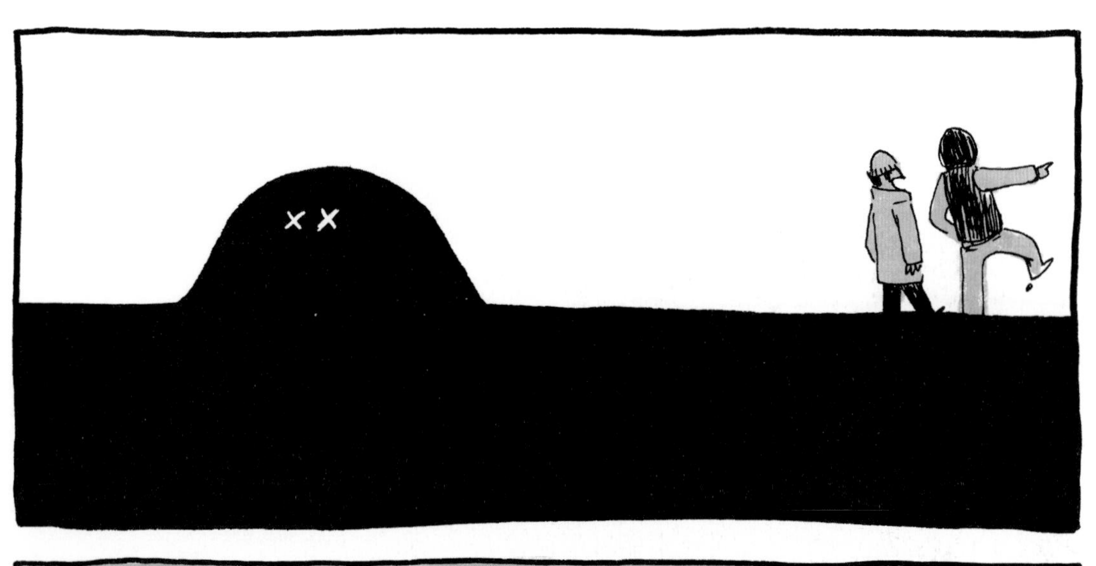

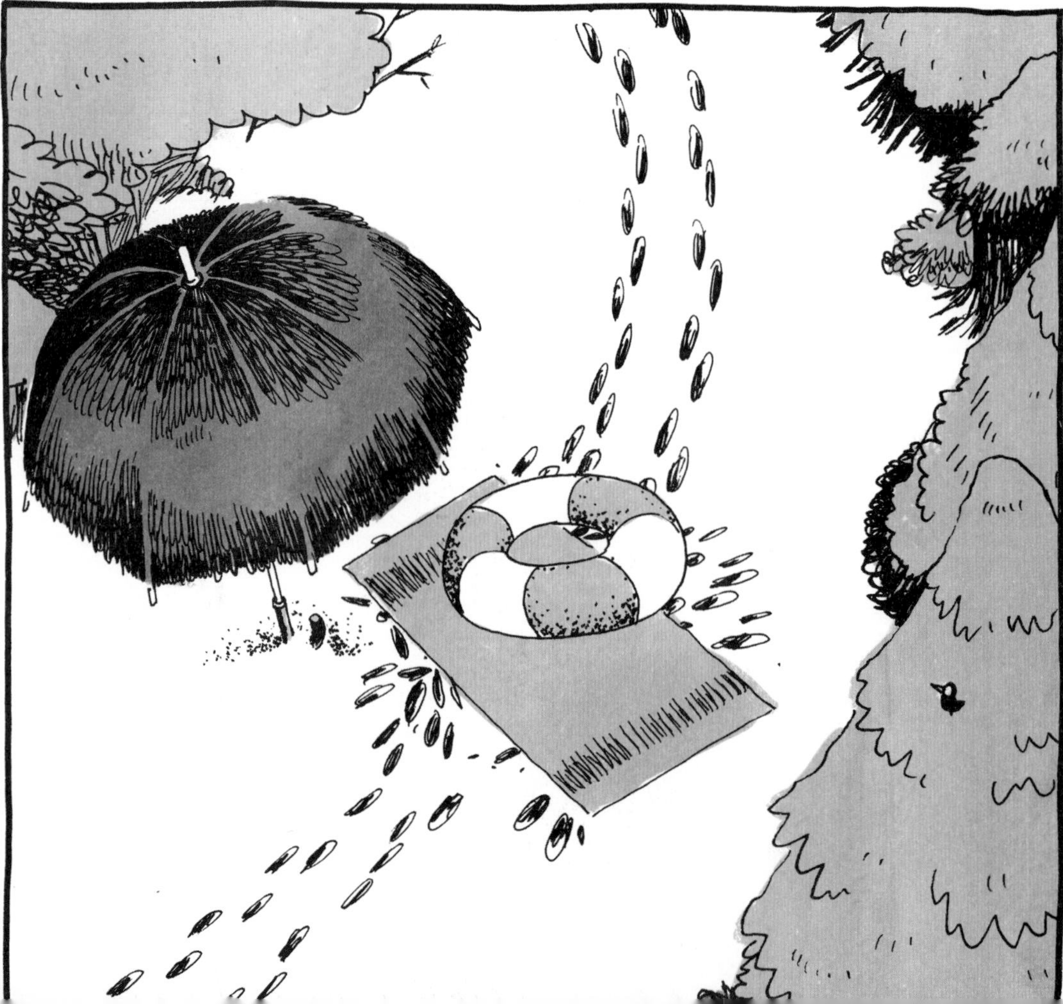

12. cat on guard

I CAN'T HANDLE HOW MUCH I LOVE CATS.
HMM...

ONE DAY, I'LL BE HIS OWNER.
NO MATTER WHAT!
LIKE THAT STRAY I LIKE IN PARTICULAR THAT COMES INTO THE CORRIDOR.
...HE'S SO MYSTERIOUS I HAVEN'T EVEN MET HIM YET.

OH, WHAT A JOY IT WOULD BE, IF WE COULD LIVE A HAPPY LIFE TOGETHER....
SUCH A WONDERFUL LIFE!

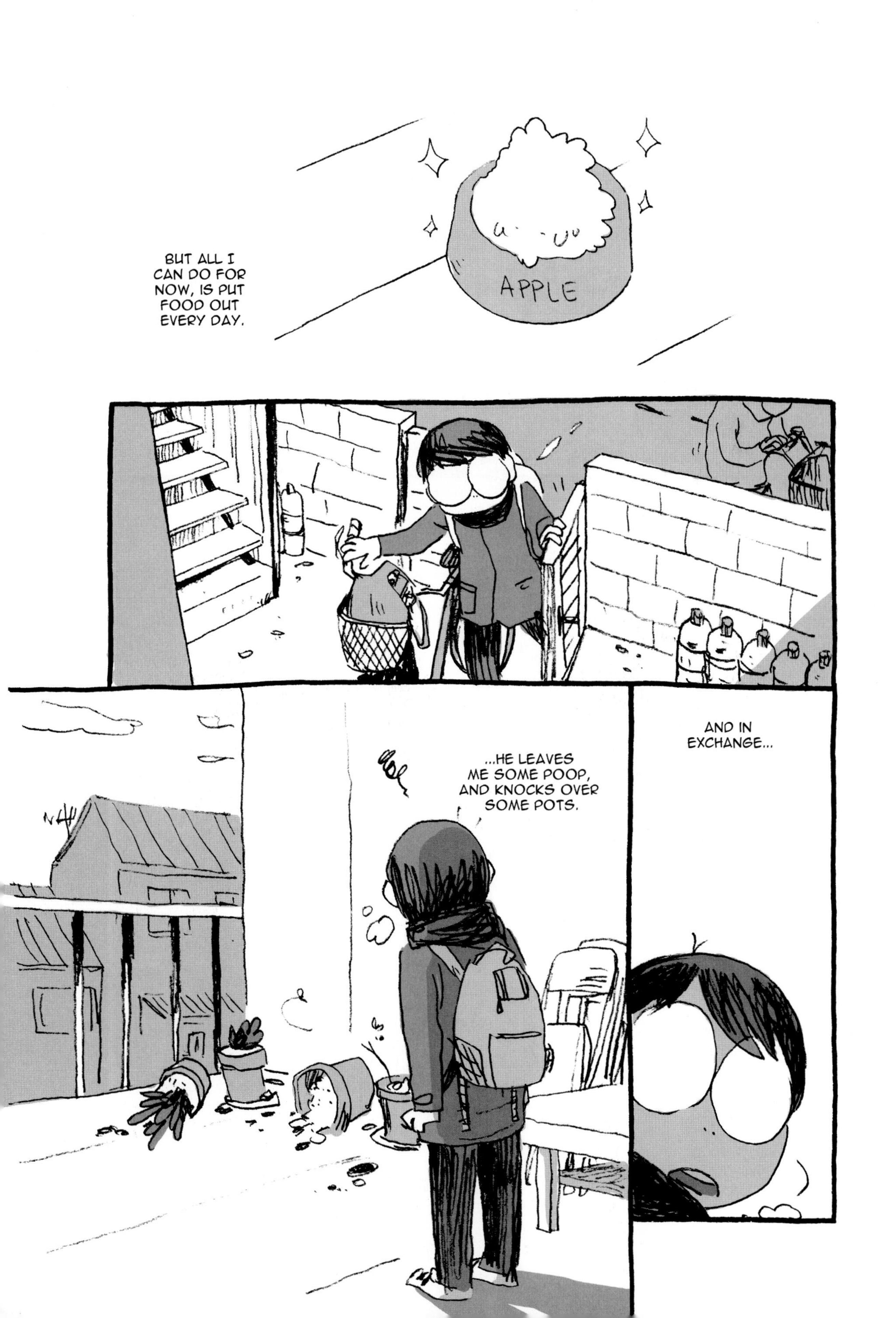
BUT ALL I CAN DO FOR NOW, IS PUT FOOD OUT EVERY DAY.
APPLE
...HE LEAVES ME SOME POOP, AND KNOCKS OVER SOME POTS.
AND IN EXCHANGE...

NO MATTER HOW MANY TIMES I CLEAN IT UP,
HE ALWAYS MAKES A MESS.
BUT I FIND IT ENDEARING.
I ALSO STRONGLY BELIEVE...
YOU COULD SAY IT'S OUR OWN SECRET LANGUAGE.

...THAT THERE'S A DEEPER MEANING TO HIS RECKLESSNESS.
SWAT
SWAT

ブー
BRRR...
OH!
WHOA
キイイイイイ
SCREECH!
THAT WAS...
CLOSE...

CLICK
I APOLOGISE FOR THE LATE DELIVERY.
NO NO,
THAT'S FINE.
I'M...
SO... SORRY...
I THOUGHT YOU WEREN'T COMING ANYMORE!
タッ
RUN
タッ
RUN
タッ
RUN

OH!
CLANG
I'M GOING TO TREAT MYSELF TO CAKE!
LET'S GO TO TEA.
THANK GOD...
WHAT IS WRONG WITH YOU?!
S... SORRY MA'AM!
...KIND OF LIKE THAT.

IT MIGHT LOOK LIKE HE'S JUST GETTING INTO MISCHIEF...
BUT HE'S PROTECTING THIS CITY.

THAT'S WHY, IF I BECOME HIS OWNER,
...HE'LL PROTECT ME TOO!

YEAH... WELL...
ALL HE DOES IS CAUSE TROUBLE, RIGHT?
UH... YOU SHOULD LAY OFF THE VIDEO GAMES.
WHAT'S THAT SUPPOSED TO MEAN?
THERE WASN'T A SINGLE POSITIVE SIDE TO YOUR STORY.
HATE TO SAY IT, BUT YOU'RE DELUSIONAL.
RIGHT.

OK, GOOD NIGHT!
SEE YA!

THEY MIGHT HAVE A POINT...
BANG

MEOW
OWW...
OH!
JUMP
AND THAT'S WHEN I DECIDED...
I WOULDN'T BECOME A CAT OWNER.
WHAAAT?

LOOKS LIKE YOU FINALLY UNDERSTAND THE TRUE CHARACTER OF CATS.
GONNA GO WITH A DOG INSTEAD? HAHA!
THAT'S NOT IT.
CRASH!
ACTUALLY...
ARE YOU ALRIGHT?
I'M SO SORRY, IT WAS ALL MY FAULT!

SOME-
BODY
CALL THE
COPS!
THE...
THE
BRAKES!
SWISH

I REALIZED I NEED
TO LET HIM BE FREE.

I CONFESS NOT HAVING MY VERY OWN CAT MAKES ME A BIT SAD...

...BUT WHEN I THINK ABOUT IT...

I CAN IMAGINE
THE CATS OF THE
WORLD AS MY PETS,
AND THAT MAKES
ME WAY HAPPIER.

HIC
... AND THAT MAKES ME WAY HAPPIER.
YEAH, YEAH!
DUDE, YOU'RE OBNOXIOUS WHEN YOU DRINK.
OH YEAH? HAHA!
THAT'S ENOUGH BOOZE FOR YOU!
HEY!
GIVE ME BACK MY **PLUM WINE!**
COME AND GET IT!
WOO HOO!

13. shut up

CONGRATULATIONS
TO US

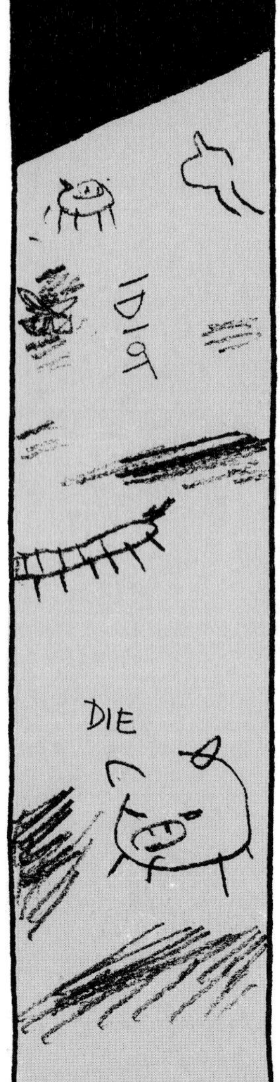
IDIOT
DIE

DIE

STUPID
GO BACK

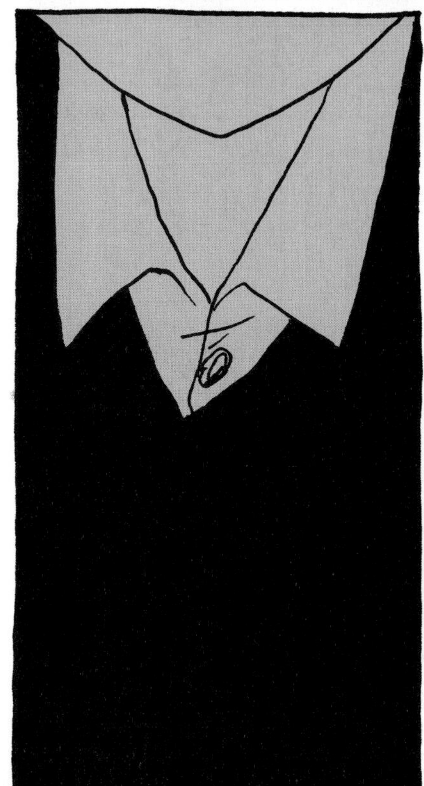

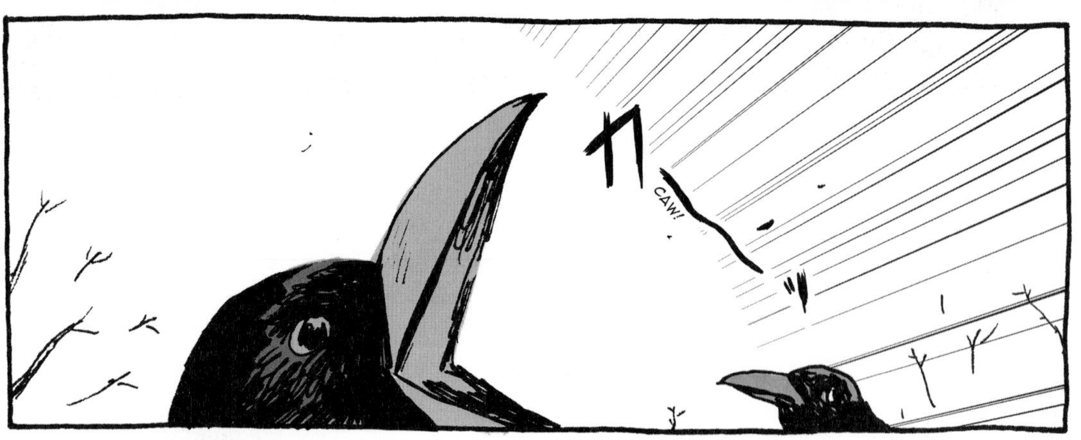

*GRADUATION CEREMONY

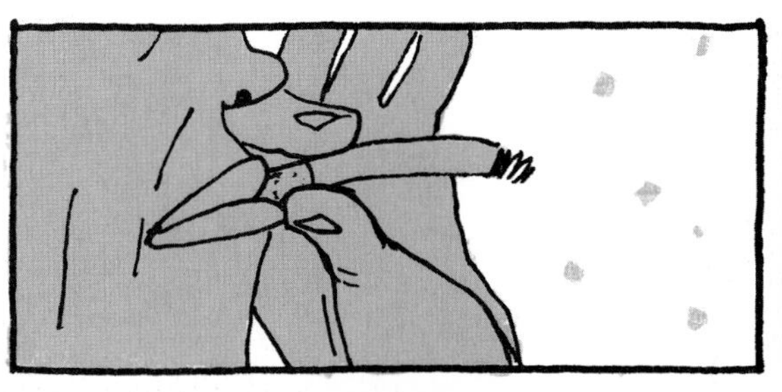

HEY.

CONGRATS, NAT-CHAN! YOU GRADUATED!

I'M SO SORRY.

YOU KNOW YOUR AUNT'S ALWAYS HAD A BAD ATTITUDE.

BUT SHE ONLY GETS UPSET BECAUSE SHE WORRIES ABOUT YOU.

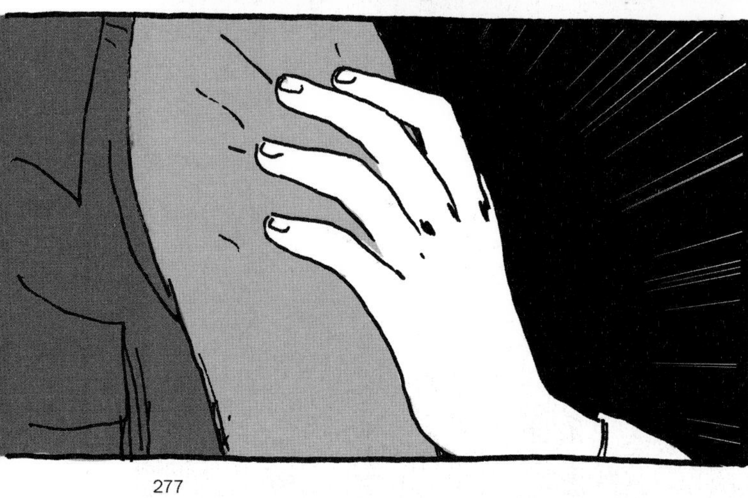

SO,
NAT-CHAN, YOU SURE YOU'RE PREPARED?

I TOLD YOU I WASN'T WORKING TODAY.
DAMN IT!
SCUFFLE

SLAM!

COME ON, WE'RE GOING.
SCUFFLE

SAY HI TO EVERYONE BACK HOME FOR ME.

THERE YOU ARE!

YOU DISAPPEARED ALL OF A SUDDEN, SO...

THANK GOODNESS!

HERE.

THANKS FOR HAVING MY BACK THE ENTIRE YEAR.

...AND I'M SORRY I COULDN'T SAVE YOU THE WAY YOU SAVED ME...

THE TRAIN IS NOW DEPARTING.

NAT-CHAN.

OH...
WELL, TAKE CARE... THEN.

YOU'LL BE FINE
THERE NOW,
WON'T YOU?

YOU'RE WELCOME
BACK ANYTIME.

ザザ
SCUFFLE
ザザ
SCUFFLE

バサ
SCUFFLE
バサ
SCUFFLE
ザ
ザ
SCUFFLE

NA-...

NAT-CHAN, YOU SNEAKY LITTLE...

henshin - the end

words and drawings
ken niimura

editor
yumetaro toyoda

translation
ivy yukiko ishihara oldford

special thanks
chris butcher
joe kelly
takeshi miyazawa
miho ota
emma rios

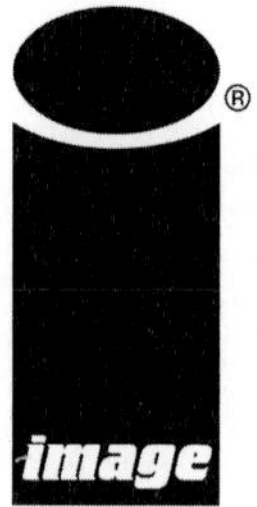

For international rights, contact: sakai@madlead.jp. ISBN: 978-1-63215-242-8